camp❀ CONFIDENTIAL

Freaky Tuesday

GROSSET & DUNLAP
Published by the Penguin Group
Penguin Group (USA) Inc., 375 Hudson Street,
New York, New York 10014, U.S.A.
Penguin Group (Canada), 90 Eglinton Avenue East, Suite 700, Toronto,
Ontario, Canada M4P 2Y3 (a division of Pearson Penguin Canada Inc.)
Penguin Books Ltd, 80 Strand, London WC2R ORL, England
Penguin Ireland, 25 St Stephen's Green, Dublin 2, Ireland
(a division of Penguin Books Ltd)
Penguin Group (Australia), 250 Camberwell Road, Camberwell, Victoria 3124,
Australia (a division of Pearson Australia Group Pty Ltd)
Penguin Books India Pvt Ltd, 11 Community Centre, Panchsheel Park,
New Delhi - 110 017, India
Penguin Group (NZ), 67 Apollo Drive, Rosedale, North Shore 0745,
Auckland, New Zealand (a division of Pearson New Zealand Ltd)
Penguin Books (South Africa) (Pty) Ltd, 24 Sturdee Avenue, Rosebank,
Johannesburg 2196, South Africa

Penguin Books Ltd, Registered Offices:
80 Strand, London WC2R ORL, England

Cover designed by Ching N. Chan.
Front cover image © PhotoAlto Photography/Student Campus/Veer Inc.

Library of Congress Control Number: 2007009630

ISBN 978-0-448-44651-6   10 9 8 7 6 5

camp CONFIDENTIAL

Freaky Tuesday

by Melissa J. Morgan

Grosset & Dunlap

Posted by: Brynn
Subject: Heeelp!!!!

My whole life has been flipped upside down.
No, make that my whole WORLD. And I'm not just
being my usual drama girl self. Really. First, I get
home from camp and I have a whole different house.
My parents moved over the summer. Without telling
me. They said they thought it would be a—note the
quotes—"fun surprise." Hello. Surprises are excellent
for birthdays, not major life changes.

Actually, after I got over the shock—Hey,
that's what my parents should have called it. A "fun
shock." Anyway, after I adjusted, I decided the new
place is pretty cool. It's not that far away from where
we used to live. And my new room—it has shutters
on the inside. Cute white shutters. I LOOOOVE them.
They are so much more original than curtains or
blinds. And my parents are letting me redecorate.
I'm getting one of those beds that has curtains
draped all around it. Not a canopy. But like a gauzy
tent. And yes, I know I just basically said curtains

are uncool. But that's just on windows. Around a bed—they're fabulous!

Anyway, the new house with the new room and the new furniture is only part of the life flipping. I'm also going to a new school. A private one, with uniforms and everything. Confession—I'm scared!!!

I've never been the new girl before. I know I'm not exactly shy or anything, but I have a little case of the wiggins thinking about walking into my first class not knowing anybody. As in ANYbody. Have any of you ever been the new girl? If you have, heeelp! I need survival tips. Who do I sit with at lunch on the all-important Day One? Am I supposed to start up conversations with people before classes start? Or do I wait and let them talk to me first, since I'm the newb? What if I get lost and have to walk into class late? What do I say? Please advise.

And that advising, I need it fast, fast, fast. 'Cause I have to start at my new school the Tuesday after Labor Day. I always thought private schools started later. So please, please, please answer before then.

Brynn stared at her computer screen, willing one of her Camp Lakeview buddies to post an answer on the camp's two-bunk blog. Maybe Grace. She was always so calm and rational. Or Natalie. She'd walked down the red carpet with her dad at actual Hollywood movie premieres. She'd definitely know how to handle a minor social situation like dealing with a new school.

You were popular at your old school. You'll be popular at your new school, Brynn told herself. But she still wanted the assist from her friends. Just to be on the safe side.

She checked her computer to see if any answers had come in during the fourteen seconds since she'd posted her message. Nope. Maybe it was time to shoot Jordan a quick e-mail as well.

To: imnotmichaelJORDAN@rcn.com
From: Brynnwins@pc.com
Subject: New Girl Syndrome

Hey Jordan,
    I'm on the verge of freaking. What if no one at my new school likes me? What's a (new) girl to do?
    XO Brynn

Brynn clicked back on the message board. Maybe that would distract her. There was a new message from Gaby Parsons. Gaby wasn't her favorite Camp Lakeview girl. But Gaby did have a snarky sense of humor. She'd probably have something entertaining to say. Brynn started to read.

Posted by: Gaby
Subject: Sainthood

This goes out to everyone who lives around Philadelphia. I'm going to be volunteering at the Home Away From Home center near the Children's Hospital and I wanted to know if any of you would like to volunteer with me. Home Away From Home is a place where the families of sick kids can stay while the kids are in the hospital.
    I decided that this year I want to spend more time

thinking about other people. That whole situation at camp where I sort of fibbed to all of you? Okay, I mean I told you big fat lies. That time? The way you were all so nice to me afterward made me think that maybe I should try to be a little nicer. So what do you say? I'll be in charge and get things organized. Come on, don't you want to be good like me? From now on, I expect you all to call me Saint Gabrielle.

Huh, Brynn thought. *Good for Gaby.* Brynn's world had been shaken up by her parents' decision to move and to put Brynn in a private school. But Gaby was shaking up her own life because she wanted to be a better person. That was pretty cool.

Brynn did a check for new messages again, because now it had been more than a minute since she'd posted her plea for heeelp. And this time there were two—one from Valerie and one from Alex. Brynn read Valerie's first.

Posted by: Valerie
Subject: Chill

Brynn, don't be stressing. You HAVE been the new girl once already, and it went great! Think about it—you were the new girl your first year at camp. We all were newbs. We didn't even know why you shouldn't eat the meat loaf. And we came away from our first summer with tons of BFFs. Look at us. We're all hanging out on the blog, keeping in touch. So I repeat, there's no need for stress!

P.S. Milo Ventimiglia rocks my socks!

Good point, Brynn thought. *We were all new girls at camp. And camp turned out so fun!* Already feeling better about her first day as the New Girl, Brynn moved on to Alex's post.

Posted by: Alex
Subject: Brynn Friends

I have advice, Brynn. I have the perfect advice. All you have to do is join the drama club. You're so talented. They're going to be so happy to have you as soon as they see you do your stuff. I bet after one meeting you'll have more friends at your new school than you can handle. That's how it was for me once I started joining sports clubs.
Good luck! And you better not forget about me when all those new friends of yours are always calling you!

By the time she finished reading Alex's message, a post from Grace had popped up on the board. Her camp friends were *so* coming through for her!
She used the mouse to click on Grace's post and started to read.

Posted by: Grace
Subject: Drama Queens Rule (tee hee)

Of course drama club is the answer! We both know how tight drama people are. You'll have oodles of friends in days.

I gotta go. It's garbage night and my mom is yelling for me to take out the trash. If you are still feeling stressed, do what I do—eat twelve purple gummy bears. Yes, they have to be purple or it won't work.

Brynn smacked herself on the forehead. Alex and Grace were so right! Brynn already had friends at the new school. Drama friends. They just hadn't met her yet. And she hadn't met them. But they were still her friends. Once she met them, they'd introduce her to their non-drama friends, and Wilton Academy popularity, here Brynn came.

▲ ▲ ▲

This is SO nothing like the first day of camp, Brynn thought as she stepped through the heavy oak doors that led into the Wilton Academy. At camp, the counselors had get-to-know-you games planned. They made sure all the kids got introduced to one another, and that nobody was left out.

There were no camp counselor types here. She was on her own. *Just remember what Alex and Grace said about drama club,* Brynn reminded herself. *That will change things.*

She checked her watch. Fifteen minutes before her first class. She couldn't just stand by her locker looking like the loneliest girl on the planet. The bathroom, she decided. She could brush her hair, do a lip gloss check, and make sure the tie on her blue plaid uniform wasn't askew. That would keep her busy.

But first she had to find it. One of the other new-girl things. She didn't know where anything was. She could ask someone, but everyone seemed to be talking to somebody already, doing the catching up after summer vacay thing.

Brynn decided to just head down the hall and keep her eyes open. And before she'd reached the corner, there it was—the ladies' room. She stepped inside and headed over to the sinks. Three girls were already clustered in front of the mirrors, gabbing away.

She thought about the message Natalie had posted on the blog that morning. She'd said not to worry about who talked first. She'd told Brynn that if she felt like talking, she should just talk. *Curtain up! Showtime!* she told herself. "Hi," she said brightly as she searched her purse for her favorite peach lip gloss. "I'm new here. Just moved into the area, even though I've always lived around Boston. So what's the club situation at this school? When do they start up?"

The tallest girl gave Brynn a friendly smile. "There will be sign-up tables in the caf starting tomorrow at lunch," she answered. "What club are you thinking of?"

"Drama," Brynn answered. "I live for the stage!" she exclaimed, vamping it up for added effect. The tall girl wrinkled her nose a little. Like Brynn had let out a big smelly burp in her face.

"Do we even have a drama club here?" one of the other girls asked doubtfully, trying to straighten the knot in her tie.

How could there not be? What kind of school wouldn't

have a drama club? Brynn thought. She ran her fingers through her dark red hair, fluffing it up.

"There is one. That girl Iris was in it last year," the first girl said.

"Oh, right. Icky Iris." The third girl smoothed down her bangs and stepped away from the mirrors.

"She was upgraded," the girl who'd been fiddling with her tie jumped in. "She became Irritating Iris, remember?"

All three girls laughed. The tall girl turned to Brynn. "There's definitely a drama club."

Brynn nodded. "Thanks."

The tall girl turned back to her friends. "How many of the books on the summer reading list did you get through?"

"All of them, of course," the girl with the now-perfect tie answered.

Brynn's throat went a little dry. "Um, what class had assigned summer reading?"

"It's not for a particular class," the tall girl explained. "Each grade has a reading list. We're all supposed to read five books from it. Samantha just likes to be better than everybody else." She gave perfect-tie girl a playful slap on the shoulder.

"Like you didn't read them all," perfect-tie girl Samantha teased her back. "You're way too competitive not to have. You might end up with an A-minus or something." She glanced at Brynn. "Didn't your old school have summer reading?"

Brynn shook her head.

"I'm sure you'll be able to catch up," the tall

girl told her as she and her friends headed out of the bathroom.

Catch up? It's only day one, Brynn thought.

The first bell rang, and she hurried out of the bathroom. After Grace had taken out the trash, she'd posted another message on the blog advising Brynn how to deal if she got lost and ended up being late to class. It was advice Brynn didn't want to have to use.

She found her history classroom with a full three minutes to spare. Three minutes to start making some BFFs. Or at least Fs.

The problem was, everyone in the room was already talking to somebody else. Except one girl who was reading a massive book. Was the book something that had been on that reading list? The one Brynn knew nothing about?

Slowly, Brynn unloaded her history book, her binder, a pen, and a pencil from her backpack. Carefully, she arranged them on her desk. That had taken—not even an entire minute.

Now what? Everyone was still talking—or reading. Brynn's face started to feel like a mask.

She forced a smile. Then immediately turned the corners of her lips down. What kind of loser sat around smiling into space? Except frowning into space wasn't any better. That definitely wouldn't make her look like somebody it would be fun to be Fs with.

Brynn pressed her lips together, then tried to hold them in a nice, even line. For some reason the effort made her jaw ache. She wanted to waggle it back and forth, but that would look weird. Looking weird was worse than looking like somebody who wasn't any fun.

Finally, the teacher walked in and about fifteen seconds later, the second bell rang. Brynn didn't think she'd ever been so happy for class to start.

"Hello, everyone. For those of you who don't know me, I'm Ms. Owen. I know you probably all have a little case of whiplash. Yesterday was vacation. Today, school. So I thought we'd kick things off with something fun. A few rounds of History Bowl." She clapped her hands. "Volunteers for team captain."

Every single hand in the room—except Brynn's—went up.

"Okay, let's go with Eve and Peter," Ms. Owen said.

"I get Colin," a boy Brynn assumed had to be Peter called out.

"No fair!" the other captain, Eve, shot back. "Colin even sleeps with the History Channel on."

"You get the next pick, Eve," Ms. Owen told her. Eve scanned the room quickly. "Maddy."

"Good choice," the guy behind Brynn muttered. "I live next door to Maddy, and she spent all summer making flash cards."

You're kidding me, Brynn thought. *All summer? Who does that?*

"I made flashcards, too," the girl who'd been reading commented.

I guess that answers my question, Brynn thought.

Peter and Eve kept calling out names. And

suddenly it hit Brynn that she was going to be the last kid picked.

It doesn't mean anything, she told herself. *How could either of them pick you? They don't even know your name.*

Suddenly, Eve pointed to her.

"What's your GPA?" Eve asked.

"Umm . . ." Brynn stuttered. She wasn't exactly sure. She'd never bothered to figure it out.

"Eve, that question was not appropriate," Ms. Owen said firmly.

"I'll take Rick," Eve decided.

Peter looked around the room. Brynn knew she was the only one who hadn't been chosen. It took him a second longer. "I'll take—"

"Brynn," she supplied.

"Great," the boy behind her muttered. "Couldn't have been anything decent or she would have said."

🛖 🛖 🛖

At least there's one place where GPA and what books you've read—or haven't—don't matter, Brynn thought as she stepped into the cafeteria.

As she moved through the food line, grabbing a taco and a fruit salad, she promised herself that she was going to talk to at least one person before lunch was over. But which person? She scoped out the tables, deciding against the ones that were already almost full. The ones that were basically empty didn't seem right either. There had to be a reason they were avoided, right?

She picked one that was about half full and had

a couple kids she recognized from her morning classes sitting at it, including the girl who'd been reading the massive book before history. "Hi," Brynn said as she took one of the empty seats. She got "hi's" from pretty much everyone except one boy, who just grunted. He was already working on his homework as he shoveled food into his mouth.

"I'm Brynn. I just started here," she offered.

"Cool," the book girl said. Then she pulled out her ginormous book and started to read.

"How's everybody's first day back starting out?" Brynn asked no one in particular.

This time she got grunts from everyone. They were all either reading or scribbling away on homework as they ate. This was craziness.

There has to be a table that's more fun, Brynn thought. She looked around the room.

Her jaw dropped open. She didn't believe what she was seeing. It couldn't be possible.

She leaned forward and squinted. "This is just too bizarre," she whispered. No one at her table even bothered to ask her what she was talking about.

Brynn grabbed her backpack and her lunch tray and stood up. She needed a much closer look. "Bye, you guys," she said, and got some grunts back.

Her day seemed like it was going to turn around. There was actually somebody she knew at this school! Somebody who was already a friend! Maybe not a BFF, but definitely a F.

Of all the people on earth, Candace—repeats-every-phrase-ever-uttered-to-her Candace—was sitting at a table about twenty feet away. Never mind that she and Brynn had never actually passed the acquaintance stage. Brynn raced over to her as if they were long-lost friends and waited for a pause in the group conversation.

"You run for president, and I'll run for vice president," Samantha, the girl who had been fiddling with her tie in the bathroom, told Candace. "We'll be unstoppable. And if you hold a class office in middle school, it's easier to do it in high school. People just see you as a leader. And being a class officer in high school is great college-application material."

"I'd vote for the two of you," a cute blond boy said.

Suddenly, a realization hit Brynn. Candace was one of the popular kids. Capital P popular. Talk about bizarre. Shy, awkward, Candace. And not just plain old popular. *Class president* popular.

"I'd vote for you too, Candace," Brynn volunteered, jumping into the conversation.

Candace looked over her shoulder and her eyes widened. "Brynn!"

Samantha raised her eyebrows. "Do you two know each other?"

"We go to the same camp," Brynn explained. "And now we go to the same school, too!"

"You're going to school with me?" Candace said, doing a little of her echo thing.

"Yep," Brynn answered. She waited for Candace to ask her to sit down. There was one empty seat.

But Candace just kept looking at her.

"Anyway, I just wanted to say hi," Brynn finally said lamely. "I'll see you around." She gave a little wave to the group. Then she walked away, trying to decide if she should go back to the table of grunters or find a *new* new place to sit.

Is there anyplace I'm going to fit in here? she asked herself.

She wasn't sure about the answer. How could she be sure of anything when Candace was one of the popular kids? The Wilton Academy was turning out to be some bizarre backward school.

How was she going to survive?

chapter

TWO

Candace let her backpack fall to the floor with a *thump* the moment she got through her front door. She felt like she'd been lugging her textbooks around for a million years—when she'd really only made it through her first day at school.

She immediately headed for the stairs. She wanted to change out of her uniform right away. It fit perfectly, but somehow it still felt tight. Candace had her tie off before she walked into her bedroom. And it felt like she could breathe again. She sucked in a deep gulp of air as she pulled off her plaid skirt. She felt like hurling it onto the floor, but she hung it neatly in her closet, followed by her plain white blouse. Then she grabbed a pair of jeans and her favorite Camp Lakeview T-shirt.

Wearing the shirt made her think of camp. Had she really just been there, swimming in the lake, going on moonlit hikes, eating hot dogs at cookouts? It was hard to believe. She sat down in front of her computer to check the camp blog.

Maybe Brynn would post a message about her first day. Candace was curious to hear what Brynn thought about the Wilton Academy.

She felt bad that she hadn't asked Brynn to sit at her table. But Brynn was so different from Candace's Wilton friends. They'd think she was weird. And Brynn would probably think they were weird right back. So it was probably better that Candace had kept them apart.

"So how did it go your first day back?" her older brother asked from the doorway before Candace even had a chance to log on to the board. He was barefoot and wearing the cutoffs their mother hated. Lucky. He didn't have to go back to school for a few more days. The high school started later.

"It was fine," Candace answered. She didn't want to get into details. Max was a great older brother in a lot of ways. He was willing to drive her places. He made amazing pancakes. And he always knew about the coolest YouTube videos before anyone else.

But Candace hated talking to Max about school. It was like he had a chip in his brain that Candace didn't. An accelerated-learning chip. Her parents seemed to have it, too. It's not like Candace wasn't good at school. She got As in everything except math. But she had to really put in the hours. Max just seemed to sit in class and, zap, the facts were downloaded.

Max came into the room and plopped down on Candace's bed. "So what clubs are you signing up for this year?"

"I'm still trying to decide on the right one," she

answered. "A couple of my friends are doing debate. I think Rowan is going to do the science club."

"Maybe you should go out for the Mathletes," Max suggested.

Candace shot him a sharp look. Was he making fun of her? He knew math was her worst subject. She had even needed to have a tutor last year.

He didn't look like he was teasing. And usually when Max teased her it was about something dumb, like if she loved a song he thought was bad.

"I don't know if I'm good enough for the Mathletes," Candace answered.

"That's the point. You join the Mathletes, and you get in a couple of extra hours of math practice a week. You have friends in the group, right?"

"I have friends in the group," Candace echoed. "At least I'm almost positive Allen will sign up again."

"I'm sure he would help you out if you joined," Max said. He stood up and started for the door, then turned around. "I almost forgot. I have a surprise for you."

"A surprise for me?" Candace felt a grin spread across her face.

"Yep. Let me at your computer," Max replied.

Candace stood up, and Max took her seat in front of the monitor. He tapped a few keys, and a brightly colored grid filled the screen. "I made a study schedule for you," Max announced proudly. "I was making one for myself, and I thought you might want one, too."

"Um, thanks," Candace said, trying not to sound disappointed.

"I put you down for a couple of hours of math on Sundays, 'cause I know you need extra time on it," he explained. "But if you join the Mathletes, you could probably cut that down to one. I wasn't sure if Mom and Dad were getting you a tutor this year or not. So I didn't put that on the schedule."

"They said that we would decide in a few weeks, after I had time to see how the year was starting out for me," Candace told her brother. "I'm feeling pretty good about it."

But she wasn't feeling good at all, really. Her stomach seemed to have twisted itself into a figure eight. Day one, and she was already completely stressed out.

▲ ▲ ▲

Brynn dropped her backpack on the kitchen table with a *thud*. She'd had to lug home practically every book in her locker. Day one, and she already had a ton of homework.

She poured herself a glass of pomegranate-grape juice—way better than the bug juice at camp. *Math homework first*, she decided. Her brain was still tired after the school day, and math was her easiest subject. After math, she'd take a little break and check out the camp blog.

Time to fire up the laptop, Brynn thought twenty-five minutes later when she'd finished the last math problem. She signed on and immediately jumped to the Camp Lakeview site. No new messages on the board. She was about to head over to Little Fluffy Industries, the site with the best online games, when Alex IM'd her. Grinning, Brynn opened the window to talk to her friend.

<SoccerLover>: So how was it?
<BrynnWins>: Alexalinda, Alexadoodle, Alex baby!! It was hideous. Horrible and hideous. But I do have some truly excellent gossip. Beg and I'll tell you.
<SoccerLover>: W8. Val just IM'd me. I'm setting up a private chat room for us. Just give me a minute.

Brynn slowly counted to thirty, and then a new window popped up on her screen inviting her to a private chat. Did she want to join? "Yes," Brynn said happily, clicking to open it up. Val and Alex were already there.

<Valfrog>: Hey, girlfriend!
<SoccerLover>: Brynn was just going to give me some juicy gossip.
<Valfrog>: Wait, I want to hear about the new school.
<BrynnWins>: It's a robot academy, that's what I've decided. All anyone talks about are GPAs and reading lists and the History Channel. At my lunch table everyone was doing homework! No one even talked to me. I hate it!
<SoccerLover>: Ouch.
<Valfrog>: Did you find the drama club?
<BrynnWins>: Club sign-ups start tomorrow.
<Valfrog>: So it'll get better tomorrow. Definitely. So what's your gossip scoop?
<BrynnWins>: Candace goes to my new school. In

fact, she's in my math class.

<SoccerLover>: That's great! So you already know someone.

<BrynnWins>: Wait, wait, wait! I didn't even get to the actual gossip part. Candace is one of the most popular kids in school.

<Valfrog>: Get out! Get all the way out!

<SoccerLover>: I think my head just exploded. Yep, there's brain goo all over my keyboard.

<Valfrog>: I'm speechless. I'm typeless! I like Candace. You know I do. But Candace and popular. That's just . . . I'm typeless.

<BrynnWins>: She's thinking about running for class president, and it seems like all the other popular peeps think she'll win no prob.

<SoccerLover>: But Candace is kind of shy. It doesn't seem like her.

<BrynnWins>: I'm telling you, at my new school, Candace isn't shy. I feel like I don't even know her!

<Valfrog>: Subject change alert. Or sort of subject change. It's still about weird camper behavior. What do you guys think about Gaby volunteering at Home Away From Home?

<BrynnWins>: Gaby. Volunteering. As they used to say on *Sesame Street*, one of these things is not like the other.

<Valfrog>: Do you think it's even serious? Or do you think she's pulling a huge scam on all of us? She'll get a bunch of us to agree to help her, then just laugh and say it was all a joke. Which would be seriously twisted. We're talking about a charity that helps the families of really sick kids.

\<SoccerLover\>: But she said she's trying to change. She said what happened at camp when she lied about knowing that reality-TV guy made her think more about how she treats other people.

\<BrynnWins\>: Yeah, and even though Gaby's a tiny bit twisted, I don't think she's so twisted she'd make a joke about helping the Home Away From Home families.

\<Valfrog\>: Hmmm. I live near the Home Away From Home center. It's a great place. I'd like to volunteer there, if Gaby's not pulling a big prank. I'm going to call her up and see what I can suss out.

\<SoccerLover\>: Let us know what she says.

\<BrynnWins\>: Yeah. We require the deets.

\<Valfrog\>: You got it. L8tr.

▲ ▲ ▲

Valerie logged off the computer and pulled the Camp Lakeview contact sheet out of the top drawer of her dresser. She ran her finger down the list of names. There it was. Gaby Parsons.

Val had mixed feelings about Gaby. She could be bossy and her sense of humor could be on the mean side sometimes. But she had also totally apologized about lying to them all. She'd had the guts to admit she was wrong.

And wanting to gather volunteers for Home Away From Home—that was a really excellent thing to do. *If* Gaby was serious about it. Val quickly dialed Gaby's number before she could change her mind.

"Talk to me," Gaby said instead of hello. Her

tone was a little . . . superior.

Remember what Brynn and Alex told you. Gaby's trying to change, Val thought. *Give her a chance.*

"Hey, Gab. It's Valerie," Val said.

"Oh," Gaby said. It wasn't exactly a friendly sound. Actually, it sounded like Gaby was trying to remember who Val was.

Why am I doing this again? Val asked herself. *Oh, right. Home Away From Home is a great place and I want to help them out!*

"From camp," Val added.

"Oh! Val! Sorry," Gaby said in a rush. "I thought you were this girl Valerie from school. I couldn't figure out why she was calling me. We're in the same English class this year, but we hardly every talk. Probably because all she ever wants to talk about is Justin Timberlake. She should just change her name to Loser, right?" Gaby sucked in a breath. "Oh, wait. That wasn't nice. And I am trying to be nice. It's my new thing."

"That's why I'm calling," Val answered. "I read your message on the camp board—"

"And you want to volunteer with me?" Gaby finished for her.

"So . . . it isn't a joke?" Valerie asked. She figured she should just get her big worry out there.

"A joke? No. How would it even be a joke?" Gaby asked. Then she let out a long sigh. "Oh, I get it. Because selfish, horrible Gaby would never actually want to help anybody."

I hurt her, Valerie realized. "No. I—" She couldn't think of what to say. She *had* doubted Gaby's motives.

"Look, I really want to volunteer with you. I think it's a great idea."

"Good. I'll arrange everything. There's an orientation on Saturday. I'll e-mail you the details. And guess what? I already have another volunteer! Chelsea!"

Chelsea. Who tied with Gaby for being the most irritating girl at Lakeview. What have I gotten myself into? Val thought.

Remembering her promise to Brynn and Alex, she got back online and started to write an e-mail.

To: Brynn and Alex
From: Valerie
Subject: Freaky Tuesday

I've decided that from now on, we should refer to this day in history as Freaky Tuesday. Because one, this is the day we discovered that Candace is popular. And two, this is the day that I confirmed Gaby is absolutely sincere about volunteering. Yes, Gaby is nice!

chapter

THREE

Brynn hesitated outside the cafeteria. Lunch yesterday had not been fun.

Then she remembered something that got her rushing through the big double doors. Sign-ups for clubs started today!

Oh, yeah, she thought as she saw the long tables decorated with balloons and streamers and blowups of group photos set up along all four walls. She scanned the selections. *Where is it? Where is it?*

Yep. Uh-huh. There it is. Brynn cut across the room, heading for the Wilton Academy Drama League table. She expected there to be a long line of kids waiting to sign up for the club. At her old school, the drama club was one of the most popular ones. But there was only one girl and one guy standing in front of the Drama League table.

The boy immediately turned to face her. "Hey, I'm Drew. Anything you want to know about Drama League, I can tell you. Although my friend Rosemary over there will probably try to beat me to it. She likes to be the authority on everything." He gestured to the slim Korean-American girl standing next to him.

The girl, Rosemary, wrinkled her nose at him. "Go ahead. You talk. Enjoy your moment in the spotlight." She was pretending to be offended, but Brynn could tell that she was kidding.

"The play this fall is going to be *Little Shop of Horrors*," Drew told Brynn. "Do you know it? It's a musical about a man-eating plant who will do things for the guy who grew it if the guy kills people for him."

"I've seen the movie a billion times," Brynn answered. "I love it. All the songs are so funny, especially 'Don't Feed the Plants.'"

"My parents finally told me I could only watch it once a week," Rosemary said after she added her name to the sign-up sheet. "I was watching it, like, every day this summer because Mr. Saunders gave us the heads-up that he had picked *Little Shop* for the first play this year." She brushed her thick, dark bangs away from her eyes. "Wait. You're new here, right?"

Brynn nodded. "Is it that obvious?"

"No," Rosemary replied. "It's just that I know pretty much everybody who is into drama at this school. Mr. Saunders is going to be so psyched to have a new person in the group. He runs the club. He's an English teacher, too. He's so cool."

Drew finished signing his name on the list and handed Brynn the pen. The girl sitting behind the desk smiled. "Hi, I'm Trina. I don't think there's much else I can tell you about the club. It seems like Drew and Rosemary completely filled you in."

"You can tell me where you got that amazing

green eyeliner," Brynn said as she put her name on the list. "And you can tell me when the auditions are."

"Next Monday," Rosemary said before Trina could answer. "And the eyeliner, it's called Poison. You can get it at your finer drug stores across the country. Right now it's on sale at the Rite Aid on Stevenson and Dry Creek."

Trina laughed. "True and true. I started wearing this eyeliner when I dressed up as Cleopatra for Halloween last year and never stopped."

"I love it," Brynn said. She put the pen down on the table. There was no one else waiting to sign up for drama.

"So, new girl? Want to go get food with us?" Drew asked. The question made Brynn's first day of school seem like a bad dream. Something that was over and that had never really been important.

"It's Brynn. And yes," Brynn replied. "See you later, Trina."

Grace and Alex were so right, Brynn thought as she followed Drew to the lunch line. *All I had to do was sign up for drama, and voilà, instant friends*. Who would introduce her to their friends. Who would introduce her to *their* friends.

"Let me give you the rundown on the food selection," Rosemary said.

"Rosemary is the Rundown Queen," Drew put in. "You need to know anything, I'm talking *anything*, ask Rosemary. She told me what kind of dog fit my personality when I got a puppy last year. She told me what kind of shampoo to use. She—"

"You're making me sound obnoxious." Rosemary gave the back of Drew's neck a finger flick, then grinned at Brynn. "But I will tell you that on Wednesdays, I recommend the lasagna. And although they are available every day, I recommend always avoiding the hamburgers. Except the veggie burgers, which are tasty, unless you like the veggie burgers that try to taste like meat, which the ones they have here do not."

"What did I tell you?" Drew asked over his shoulder. He turned to the woman behind the lunch counter. "I'll have the lasagna."

"He complains. But he listens to me," Rosemary commented.

"She talks way too much. But she is often right," Drew told Brynn.

"I guess that means I'll have the lasagna, too," Brynn said.

"My circle of influence widens! Yay!" Rosemary exclaimed. She got a serving of lasagna for herself and they continued through the line, then over to seats at a table behind the one where Candace and her friends were eating. "This is our table from last year," she went on. "Unofficially, of course. There are no official tables."

"She likes this table because it gives her a good view of anybody who's anybody at school, which is very important to Rosemary," a guy already sitting at the table joked.

"Eli, why oh why are you still working the faux hawk? How many times have I told you that you need a haircut that frames your face?" Rosemary asked.

"I like it," Eli answered, running his hand over the ridge of hair in the center of his head.

"Hey, we have a new Drama League member," Drew told Eli. "Her name is Brynn."

"Great! We could really use some new blood," Eli said. "Half the group from last year is in high school now."

"More parts for us," Drew answered.

"But if we don't have enough people to put on a play, how can there be parts for anyone?" Rosemary complained.

"Really? There might not be enough people for a play?" Brynn exclaimed. "That's so freaky. At my old school, we always had way too many kids who wanted to act. Every musical had a huge chorus. The stage was jammed!"

"Drama was that popular?" Eli shook his head in disbelief.

"It was one of the most popular clubs in the place," Brynn told him.

"It's not like that here. You want me to give you the rundown on popularity at Wilton?" Rosemary asked.

"No!" Drew and Eli said together.

"Absolutely," Brynn answered. She knew Candace was popular. She was really curious to know why.

Rosemary shot a satisfied smirk at the boys. "Okay. First thing to know is that here at Wilton, academic excellence equals popularity. There's huge competition over who gets the As. The academic ranks are posted the first Monday of every month on the bulletin board by the office, and there's practically a stampede. The kids who—"

"Wait. They post your ranking where everyone can see it?" Brynn demanded, horrified. It's not that she wasn't a decent student. But that was just wrong.

"Not by name," Rosemary reassured her. "Every kid is assigned a number. So nobody knows what anyone's ranking is. At least that's how it's supposed to work."

"Yeah, everyone knows who the top people are. They don't keep it a secret," Drew volunteered.

"So anyway, as I was saying, the brainiacs are at the top of Mount Popularity," Rosemary continued. "That table in front of us?" She jerked to her chin at Candace's table. "That's where you'll find the most popular kids in school."

"I actually know one of them," Brynn said. "I go to summer camp with Candace."

"You know Candace?" Drew asked, leaning forward.

"Why aren't you eating over there?" Eli asked.

Brynn felt her face get hot. Why wasn't she eating with the one person she actually knew at this school? Answer—because the one person hadn't asked her.

"Eli!" Rosemary exclaimed.

"What? I didn't mean it in a bad way," Eli protested.

"I guess . . . I don't know. Maybe sometimes camp friends are just friends at camp," Brynn explained.

"Let's talk about something really important,"

Rosemary said. "How are we going to get more people to sign up for drama? We have to get enough to put on the play, at least."

"Maybe you could talk your friend Candace into joining," Drew suggested. "If she joined, a lot of other people would, too."

"Great idea. Will you do it, Brynn?" Eli asked.

How could she say no to the first friend-type people she'd met at Wilton? "Sure, I guess," Brynn answered.

Eli and Drew stared at her.

"You guys, she doesn't have to do it now," Rosemary said. "Let her eat."

"No, it's okay." Brynn stood up. She sucked in a deep breath and walked the few steps it took to get over to Candace's table.

"Candace, can I ask you a question?" Brynn said. Everyone stopped talking and looked at her.

"Sure," Candace said. "You know everyone, right?"

Brynn shook her head, and Candace did quick intros around the table.

"So what's the question?" Rowan, the tall girl from the bathroom yesterday, asked.

Actually, my question was for my friend Candace, Brynn felt like saying. But she wasn't even sure Candace was her friend. A real friend asked you to sit at their table.

"I wanted to see if you'd be interested in signing up for drama, Candace," Brynn said. "I just joined."

"Drama, huh?" Joshua, the cute blond boy sitting

34

next to Candace, frowned. "Why not sign up for something like debate if you like being in front of people? I'm on the debate team."

"Debate is good if you like to perform," Candace chimed in.

"It's not just performing that I like. I also like having the chance to be other people. It's so much fun!" Brynn explained. "I'm sure debate is cool and everything, but it's not like you get to live another life the way you do when you're acting."

"Maybe. But you can't choose a club just for fun," Samantha said. "Well, you can. But it's better to think ahead. It's really important what kind of extracurricular activities you put on your college application."

"My older brother is always talking about how extracurricular activities are important for your application," Candace agreed.

"Yeah," Allen, a boy with dark, intense eyes, said. "Stuff from middle school doesn't go on your app, but it helps if you get started in the right groups now. I signed up for the science club this year. Statistically, ninety-three percent of the regional science fair winners were members of their school's science club."

Whoa, Brynn thought. *Rosemary was right. This really is the brainiac table. All they seem to care about are grades and school and college.*

It wasn't as if Brynn didn't care about those things. She did. But she also cared about acting. It was the best, most fun, most exciting thing she'd ever done.

"So, I guess that's a no to joining drama?" she asked Candace.

Candace nodded, and Brynn walked back to her table.

"From your face, I'm guessing the answer is no," Rosemary said.

"Candace and her friends seemed more into the academic-type clubs," Brynn answered.

"Like what? Did Candace say?" Drew asked in a rush.

Brynn shook her head. "She said her older brother told her that extracurricular activities are really important for college. They were all talking about college like it isn't a billion years away," Brynn told them. "But she didn't say what she was signing up for."

"What about at camp?" Drew pressed. "What was she into at camp?"

"You like her!" Rosemary burst out. "How did I miss that? It's so obvious. You totally like Candace!"

"Say it louder, why don't you? And the answer is no. I'm just trying to get some more members for drama," Drew muttered, the tips of his ears turning red.

"Oh, right. You're going to gather intel on every potential club member—find out what they did over their summer vacation, what other clubs they are thinking of joining, favorite foods, the color of underwear they like. Then what? Create a personalized recruitment plan to get them into drama?" Rosemary joked.

"You have a better plan?" Drew asked, his eyes locked on the piece of lasagna on his plate. "We have to do something. We barely have enough people to put on a show."

Rosemary turned to Brynn. "Isn't that cute? He's

trying to change the subject. He's not going to admit that he liiiikes her."

He does, Brynn thought. *It's so obvious.* She studied his face, trying to memorize his expression. She could use it if she ever had to play somebody who was in liiiike and being teased about it.

"Do we need to be talking about this?" Drew protested. "Or do we need to be figuring out how to get enough people in the Drama League to actually put on some plays?"

"Too bad we can't afford a commercial," Brynn commented.

Drew snorted. "Like anyone at this school has time to watch TV. Too much homework."

"What if it wasn't on TV?" Brynn asked. "What if we could do a commercial live, right here in the cafeteria?"

"All I can say is 'huh?'" Drew replied.

"I get it. And it's a great idea!" Rosemary cried. "We can do a skit that will show everybody how much fun acting is."

"Exactly!" Brynn answered. She and Rosemary were already starting to do the friend mind-reading thing, and they'd only known each other for about half an hour. That was super cool.

"Come on!" Rosemary jumped to her feet. "We have to go find Mr. Saunders and get permission." She grinned at Brynn. "I'm so glad you ended up at our school this year!"

At least somebody is, Brynn thought, shooting a look over at Candace.

▲ ▲ ▲

Candace stared at the board as Mr. Merrill wrote the next algebra problem. *Concentrate*, she told herself. That was one of her problems. At least that's what Patrick, her tutor, had told her last year. She didn't concentrate.

And he was right. It was true. But it was just because after a point she didn't understand *anything*. Not a word coming out of the teacher's mouth. Not a page of her textbook. When she got to that point, her head just refused to stay in numbers mode. She started thinking about books she'd read, or her favorite TV show, or how she might want to rearrange the furniture in her bedroom. Sometimes she even started homework for other classes in her head. She'd be mentally writing a book report for English while her math teacher made those incomprehensible noises at the front of the class.

But that was last year, she told herself. This was a new class. With a new teacher. She had a clean slate. She hadn't taken a single test or quiz yet. At this point, she could be an A student.

She needed to get an A in this class. This year, Candace wanted all As, a perfect, pretty row of them to show her parents. She wanted to prove that Max wasn't the only one who could pull it off. Candace was sure she could make that happen in all her other subjects. But math . . .

You just have to concentrate, she told herself again. Then she realized everyone was staring at her.

"What do you say? Want to give it a shot, Candace?" Mr. Merrill asked.

Candace was positive he'd already asked her the question once, and she hadn't even noticed him calling her name. At least he wasn't one of those teachers who got all sarcastic or impatient. He was just standing there, holding out a piece of chalk, like he had all the time in the world.

"Okay. Sure. I want to give it a shot," Candace answered quickly. She couldn't believe that she'd gotten so stressed about needing to concentrate that her brain had basically shut down.

Great day two, she thought as she hurried up to Mr. Merrill, took the chalk, then positioned herself in front of the board. She sucked in a deep breath and studied the problem. Her stomach began to tighten into a ball.

"The first thing you want to do is get all the Xs on one side of the equation," Mr. Merrill coached.

"Get all the Xs on one side of the equation," Candace muttered. She hated it when she did that. She was always repeating things. It was because her parents made her go to a weekend class on good study habits once. The instructors had the kids repeat all the study tips over and over again to memorize them. The class only lasted two days, but Candace had never gotten out of the habit. And it got worse when she was nervous.

"Get all the Xs on one side," she said. D'oh. She just did it again!

Don't think about that, she ordered herself. *You have to concentrate.*

"Would anybody like to come up and give Candace a hand?" Mr. Merrill asked.

She'd blown it. She'd taken so long that Mr. Merrill had decided she couldn't do the problem.

"First we should subtract X from both sides," someone said softly from behind Candace.

Candace looked over her shoulder and saw Brynn standing there.

"That's a good place to start," Mr. Merrill agreed.

Brynn gave Candace an encouraging smile. "You can begin with this side," she coached, pointing.

Candace automatically did what Brynn said. But she was so surprised that she wasn't even paying any attention to the problem. *Brynn is good at math?* Candace thought. *At camp, all she cared about was drama. Is she smart, too? That's so weird.*

Gaby stood in front of the Home Away From Home center, waiting for "her" girls to arrive. She'd already told Ms. Jeunet that she'd recruited two friends, and that she knew they would be a great addition to the team. Ms. Jeunet had sounded impressed that Gaby had taken the initiative.

Being nice isn't so hard, Gaby thought. *I don't know why everyone makes such a big deal about it.* She checked her watch. The orientation for new volunteers started in ten minutes. She really hoped Val and Chelsea weren't going to show up late. That would be so uncool. It would make Gaby look bad if *her* people didn't bother to arrive to the Home on time.

She was pulled away from her thoughts by footsteps running toward her. She turned toward the sound and saw Val dashing up the walkway, her dozens of braids flying around her face.

"Sorry, sorry, and again sorry! I know we said we'd meet up at quarter of. I had to transfer buses to get here, and the second one didn't show up forever," Val said, breathless. "Where's Chelsea?"

"She's not here yet," Gaby replied. "She's probably still in front of her mirror, making sure her eye shadow goes with her shirt. Oh. Oops. Shouldn't have said that. Sometimes the not-nice stuff just slips out."

"Yeah, sometimes I'm amazed at what I hear coming out of my own mouth," Val answered.

"If Chelsea's not here when the orientation starts, we're going in without her," Gaby decreed.

Two little kids ran around the corner of the building and stopped in front of Gaby and Val. "You're new! What are your names?" a red-haired girl of about seven asked. "And who's sick in your families? My big sister is the sick one. My brother's okay." She jerked her thumb toward a boy with red hair who looked the same age as his sister. "He's Samuel. I'm Emma."

Gaby smiled, feeling very saintly. "I'm Gaby and this is Valerie," she said. "We don't have any sick people in our families. We're here to help you."

"We're new volunteers," Valerie added.

"You have any candy?" Samuel asked.

"He's not allowed any more candy for the day," Emma said.

Samuel socked her in the arm, then ran. Emma chased after him.

"Those were two cute kids," Valerie said.

Gaby checked her watch. "We have less than a minute."

"We don't want to miss any of it. Maybe we could leave Chelsea a note on the door that says we're inside or—" Val stopped in mid-sentence. "Never mind. There she is."

Unlike Val, Chelsea didn't bother rushing over. She strolled over. And when she reached Val and Gaby, she didn't bother apologizing. *Chelsea is really the one who needs to work on her niceness levels,* Gaby thought.

"Let's get inside," Gaby said. "We're probably going to be the last ones. I hope there are some good seats left."

"Good seats? It's not a movie," Chelsea commented as Gaby opened the front door and ushered her in.

"It's better than a movie. We're helping people," Gaby primly reminded her. She scanned the large foyer and spotted a woman with a nametag that read JULIA JEUNET. "Follow me," she told Val and Chelsea.

Gaby crossed the room and held out her hand to Ms. Jeunet. "Hello. I'm Gaby Parsons. We talked on the phone. I brought my friends to the orientation." She waved in the direction of Val and Chelsea. "We're so excited about volunteering."

It felt good to have brought Val and Chelsea to the center. Ms. Jeunet must think Gaby was an ultra-good person. She hadn't just volunteered herself.

She'd brought recruits.

"And we're excited to have you here," Ms. Jeunet answered. "We're going to be meeting in the dining room. Just go on in. It's the yellow door to the left."

"It's cute how all the doors are different colors," Val said as they walked into the dining room.

"I think it would look better if they were at least all shades of the same color," Chelsea said. "And I think the chairs should match." She shook her head, looking at the mix of armchairs and straight-back chairs circling the large wooden table.

"It makes the place cozy," Val said, plopping down in the nearest armchair.

Chelsea raised her eyebrows. "What do you think?" she asked Gaby.

"I don't think the decor is important," Gaby answered, sitting next to Val. Although, actually, she agreed with Chelsea. The place did feel a little too thrown together.

She glanced around at the other people at the table. She, Chelsea, and Val were the youngest. There were a couple of girls who were maybe in college. Some mom-aged women, some in suits, some in jeans and those tacky sweatshirts with the appliqués. There weren't many guys. Just three. One who looked sort of like Santa Claus, with the white hair and the belly. And two who looked like your basic dads. No cuties.

Chelsea leaned across Val and whispered, "Is there some rule that says cute boys can't volunteer?"

"Shhh! And also, that's not why we're here," Gaby whispered back. What would everyone think if they heard that? Gaby didn't want people to think she was volunteering so she could meet cute boys. She was volunteering because she was a good person and it was a good thing to do.

"Maybe we should volunteer to hunt down some hottie volunteers," Val jumped in, keeping her voice low. "That would be a fun job!"

"You two should just leave if all you can think about is boys," Gaby snapped, forgetting to whisper. Val and Chelsea were ruining everything. Gaby had brought them with her. She had introduced them to Ms. Jeunet. So if they looked silly and shallow, it made Gaby look silly and shallow.

"Uh-oh. Does that mean I have to leave, too? I think about boys an awful lot," one of the college girls asked with a grin.

Val and Chelsea laughed.

"I didn't mean . . . I wasn't talking to you," Gaby said, embarrassed.

"All right, everyone. Let's get started," Ms. Jeunet called as she walked into the room. She sat down next to Gaby, not bothering to go to the empty chair at the head of the table.

"First I want to tell you a little bit about Home Away From Home," Ms. Jeunet continued. "It was started by Clarissa and Robert Hanson, a couple whose daughter, Shannon, had leukemia. Of course, the Hansons wanted to be with Clarissa whenever she was in the hospital. The closest motel to the Children's Hospital pretty much became their home away from home." She smiled. "Now you know where the name came from."

Gaby nodded. She already knew the background of Home Away From Home. She'd read everything on their website.

"Every once in a while, Clarissa and Robert would meet other families staying at the motel who were in the same situation. Parents who also had children in the hospital. Talking to these other parents was a huge comfort to the Hansons, and that's what gave them the idea for Home Away From Home," Ms. Jeunet explained.

Gaby wondered how many times Ms. Jeunet had told this story. It didn't sound memorized or rehearsed, but she had to have given this talk at a ton of volunteer orientations.

"They thought it would be great if there was a place close to the hospital where parents with sick kids could all stay. Someplace that was more comfortable than a motel," Ms. Jeunet went on. "Someplace where life could feel a little bit normal. With a kitchen where people could cook their own meals. And a play area where the other children in the families could hang out. And a big living room where there was always somebody to talk to."

Then Ms. Jeunet listed the different kinds of volunteers they needed at Home Away From Home. Babysitting. Gaby could hear a baby crying somewhere in the house right now. Even from this far away it was starting to make her nuts.

Grocery shopping. You needed a car for that one. And grocery shopping? Gaby bet that was the one kind of shopping even Chelsea wasn't into.

Laundry. Gaby would melt into a pool of liquid boredom.

Cataloging the books in the library. Yawn.

Organizing entertainment for the brothers and sisters of the patients. Ms. Jeunet explained that volunteers could organize a movie night, or run an afternoon of games—anything where the kids could have a good time.

That's it, Gaby decided, not bothering to listen to the rest of the list.

▲ ▲ ▲

"So what should we sign up for?" Gaby asked when the orientation ended.

"I think helping expand the playground would be tons of fun," Val answered. "I've always wanted to wear a tool belt."

"That's not a good look for anybody," Chelsea told her. "Especially anybody with hips. And anyway, we should do cooking. Every time I watch *America's Favorite Chef*, I want to start chopping something."

Gaby couldn't believe this was happening. She'd only asked them what they wanted to do to be nice. She'd been positive they would want to sign up for entertainment. It was so clearly the best job.

"What about entertainment?" Gaby looked back and forth between Chelsea and Valerie. "We'd be like camp counselors. We could come up with lots of great games and activities."

"Cooking is the best—" Chelsea began to protest.

Gaby cut her off. "We need to show the kids

how to have fun Camp Lakeview—style!" she exclaimed. "I'm signing us up for entertainment right now." She rushed over to the wall where the sign-up sheets were posted and wrote her name in big, clear letters. Then she added Valerie's and Chelsea's.

The whole volunteering thing was Gaby's idea. It was only fair that she get to choose what job they'd do.

To: Brynn and Alex
From: Valerie
Subject: The Deets

You guys said you wanted the details on how the volunteering thing went. All I can say is OMG. You should have seen Chelsea and Gaby. It was a complete Clash of the Control Freaks. I'm surprised I'm not blood spattered right now.

See, there was this list of jobs that Home Away From Home needed volunteers for. Like expanding their playground, which I thought would be cool (and I'd get to wear a tool belt!), but whatev. So Chelsea wanted to volunteer to help cook a meal, and Gaby wanted to volunteer to organize some fun activities for the brothers and sisters of the kids who were sick.

You won't believe this. Actually, you will, because you know Gaby. Anyway, Gaby just signed me, Chelsea, and herself up for the activities. And Chelsea threw a hissy. She and Gaby really got into it. Gaby only won because Chelsea's mother came to pick her up first.

I actually think planning some games and stuff for the kids would be fun. If I wasn't doing it with the Temper Twins.

There you have it.

Peace out,

Val

chapter

FOUR

"Peanuts, hard-boiled eggs, and steak strips," Candace's mother said, setting plates down on the kitchen table. "All guaranteed brain food. Do you need anything else?"

"Anything else?" Candace echoed, looking from Joshua to Samantha to Rowan—the members of her study group.

"An A on my first French quiz," Joshua joked.

Candace's mom opened the fridge and peered inside. "Sorry. Must have forgotten to put that on the shopping list. I guess you'll have to study," she said with a smile. "I'll leave you to it," she added over her shoulder as she headed out of the kitchen.

Candace glanced at the food and sighed. She would much rather have chips and pretzels like they did at camp. Who cared if snack food made your brain work better? Snack food was supposed to taste yummy and that was about it.

"Wouldn't it be cool if you could just go to the store and pick up good grades?" Rowan asked. "My parents told me they'd give me fifty dollars for every A I bring down this year. If I could buy As for thirty dollars each, I'd be making twenty bucks an A!"

Joshua laughed. "You sound like one of those word problems we had back in elementary school." His expression turned serious. "I can't believe your parents pay you for As. My parents just expect me to have a row of them on every report card. And when I do, they hardly say anything. I'd only hear about it if I did something horrifying—like get a B."

"That's sort of how it is for me," Candace said. "My parents tell me I did a good job if I get As. But they say a lot more if I don't." She thought about last year when she'd brought home a B-minus in math. She'd definitely heard about that. It wasn't that her parents had yelled or anything. But the three of them—and sometimes Max, too—had long talks about motivation, study skills, and homework schedules. For a while, it had felt like math was her whole world. That's why it had been extra great to get to camp this year and just forget about school for a while.

"What about you, Samantha?" Joshua asked. "Are your parents bribers or yellers or what?"

"They think school is my job," Samantha answered. "They say I'm old enough to know that actions have consequences. Studying hard means you get As. Slacking off means you don't. My parents think that decision is mine."

Joshua snorted. "Yeah, right. I bet that would change the second you brought home a B."

"Samantha doesn't do Bs," Rowan reminded everyone.

Samantha tossed her head, sending her long, long hair flying. "Can I help it if I'm naturally brilliant?" she asked.

She was incredibly smart. But Candace knew that Sam worked hard to get the grades she did.

"You know who's truly naturally brilliant?" Rowan asked. "Allen. That boy never studies. I mean it. Never. And he's still in the top ten every month when the rankings are posted."

"He's in the top ten every month," Candace agreed. Then she winced, realizing she'd slipped into the repeating thing again.

"I know. I hate him," Joshua joked. But there was an edge to his voice. He wasn't completely kidding.

That's so weird, Candace thought. *Joshua and Allen have been best friends since kindergarten.*

She managed to keep herself from repeating anything Joshua said. There was no reason for the nervous habit now. She was hanging in her own kitchen with her friends. It's just that all the talk about rankings and As made her think of math. And that stressed her out.

"If Allen actually did study, he'd give you some real competition for the number-one ranking," Rowan told Samantha.

Samantha did another hair toss. "You're saying Allen is smarter than me?"

"Than I," Joshua corrected with a smile.

"We're not working on English right now," Samantha shot back.

"What are we going to start with?" Candace asked quickly. She felt like the conversation could turn ugly any second. When had her friends become so competitive? She didn't like the tension in the room. And besides, they needed to get to work.

But Samantha ignored the question. "Speaking of English, did I tell you guys that the short story I wrote over the summer is going to be in the school paper on Friday?"

"How did you swing that?" Rowan asked. "You aren't even on the newspaper staff."

"Mr. Kinney knew I went to writing camp over the summer. He asked to see some of my stuff. He really liked one of the stories, so he asked me if they could run it in the paper," Samantha explained.

"That's not exactly fair," Rowan commented. "He should have asked everyone if they had stories they wanted considered. It's not like you have to go to writing camp to write."

"What should we start with?" Candace asked again. She had the feeling the issue of whether or not Mr. Kinney should have gotten stories from everyone could turn into a debate. A loooong one.

"How about math?" Joshua suggested.

"How about math?" Candace repeated. She couldn't stop herself.

▲ ▲ ▲

Drew dumped a box of Pop-Tarts, a bag of Chips Ahoy, and a bag of mini candy bars on the kitchen table. "What?" he asked as Brynn and Rosemary stared at the pile of junk food. "I run on sugar. You can't expect me to come up with a skit without it."

"The only thing is, I run on grease. And salt," Rosemary told him.

Drew shot her a grin, then pulled a large bag of Doritos out of the cupboard and added it to the pile. He turned to Brynn. "Anything you need to help you think?"

"I'm flexible. I can run on either sugar or salty grease." She grabbed one of the chocolate chip cookies and a handful of the Doritos.

"Did you know that Doritos are made in York County, Pennsylvania?" Rosemary asked. "It's called the Snack Capital of America because there are so many snack-food makers there."

"You really are the queen of useless knowledge," Drew told her. "So what arc we going to do for our skit? How are we going to make everyone want to sign up for drama?"

"We have to make acting look like fun," Brynn said. "Which shouldn't be that hard. Acting *is* fun."

"Why is acting fun? Maybe that's what we should think about for starters," Rosemary said. She licked the salt off a chip and smacked her lips.

"The applause," Brynn joked. Mostly joked. She did love hearing a crowd give it up for her. But that was only a teeny part of why she wanted to act.

"Getting to learn new stuff," Drew offered. "Like fencing. Or how to do magic, like when I played Houdini."

"I like how extreme you get to be," Rosemary

said. "I played Helen Keller in *The Miracle Worker* once. I loved throwing those huge tantrums. It's fun being able to do stuff you'd never get away with in real life."

"Oooh, that gives me an idea!" Brynn exclaimed. "What if we did a skit where we were, like, the Dramatics. The most dramatic family on the planet. If one of the Dramatics forgot to say 'good morning,' one of the other ones would burst out sobbing. I'm talking big-time tragedy."

"And the other one could get furious. And just go off like a maniac off his meds," Drew added.

"Exactly!" Brynn exclaimed.

They both looked over at Rosemary. Her eyes had gone so wide that white showed all around her irises. She wrapped her arms tightly around herself, but she couldn't stop shivering.

"What's wrong?" Brynn demanded.

Rosemary leaned forward and whispered, "I love this idea so much it scares me."

Drew cracked up. So did Brynn. *These are sooo my peeps*, she thought.

"Great. So our skit will be about the Dramatics," Drew decreed.

It's going to be fab, Brynn thought. She couldn't wait for lunch on Friday. She couldn't wait to perform the skit for everybody in school. They were going to love the Dramatics—and Brynn!

▲ ▲ ▲

"Looks good, tater tot," Chelsea's father said as he came into the kitchen.

"Don't call me tater tot," she said automatically, even though she didn't really mean it. She studied the plates of snacks in the middle of the kitchen table, then nodded. "They do look good, don't they?" The garnishes of sliced bell peppers set off the sunshine yellow plates perfectly.

"Good enough to eat," her dad said. He grabbed a bottle of water out of the fridge and left the kitchen.

Chelsea turned her attention back to the table. The bruschetta smelled so good, she felt like gobbling it all up before Val and Gaby arrived. Not that she'd ever do that. Messing with the perfectly rounded mound of bruschetta would throw the whole display out of balance. Gaby probably didn't care about things like that. And Valerie was too laid back to notice. But Chelsea liked perfection.

In fact . . . she hurried to the bathroom and did a quick makeup and hair check. She was glad she had. The thickness of her eye shadow was slightly out of balance. She grabbed a tissue and ran it lightly over her left eyelid. Yes. Perfect.

The doorbell rang, and Chelsea smiled. She couldn't wait to tell the other girls her plan for the Home Away From Home activity night. It was, what was the word? Her smile stretched into a grin. Perfect. She still thought it would be more fun to cook dinner for everyone at the center. But since Gaby had had a tantrum and insisted on doing the activities, Chelsea had come up with the best idea for what they should do. She wasn't afraid of teamwork, and now Gaby would know that.

The doorbell rang again as Chelsea walked down the hall. *That has to be Gaby,* she thought. *Valerie's not that impatient.*

She was right. She saw Gaby standing on her porch though one of the diamond-shaped panes of glass in the front door. *I would have gone a different way with the accessories,* Chelsea told herself, taking in Gaby's topaz earrings paired with a topaz pendant *and* a topaz bracelet.

But all she said when she opened the door was, "Interesting jewelry." Gaby wasn't the only one who could be saintly.

"Thanks," Gaby answered. She thrust a greasy paper bag into Chelsea's hands. "I brought snacks, these cookies my mom came up with."

Chelsea peeked into the bag. The cookies were practically blinding. They were bright green with gobs of M&Ms in the center. Did she have to put them out? They would completely ruin the arrangement she'd made on the table. "Um, why are they green?" She knew it wasn't the most polite question, and she'd really been trying hard to be polite lately, but she had to ask.

"They're supposed to look like birds' nests," Gaby answered. "The M&Ms are the eggs."

"But why green?" Chelsea pressed. "Aren't nests brown?" Not that that would be much better. It would help a little, though.

"Nests can be made of grass—green grass," Gaby reminded her. "I have something else for you, too." She handed Chelsea an orange folder.

"What's—" Chelsea began. The beep-beep of a

car horn interrupted her. She peered over Gaby's shoulder and saw Valerie climbing out of a VW Bug.

"Hey, we got here at the same time," Valerie said to Gaby. "That's a whatchamacallit? A good omen. We're going to have an awesome planning session."

"Definitely," Gaby said. "This is for you." She handed Valerie an orange folder like the one she'd given Chelsea.

"What is it?" Valerie asked as she and Gaby stepped into the entryway.

"It's everything we need to have the ultimate scavenger hunt at Home Away From Home," Gaby answered.

Chelsea froze, not even finishing closing the door behind them. "What?" she managed to get out.

"I have maps of the whole house, all three of the main floors, plus the basement and the attic. I went over there and drew them myself. The place is big enough to do the whole hunt inside," Gaby explained. "I already made lists of possible objects to search for. Or I guess I should say scavenge for."

"A scavenger hunt could be fun," Valerie said, flipping open her folder.

Chelsea's hand tightened on the doorknob. She couldn't believe this was happening. Gaby had totally gotten her way about doing activities instead of cooking or . . . whatever that thing Val wanted to do was. And now she thought she could plan the activity entirely by herself? Did she really think she got to run the whole thing with Chelsea and Valerie as her little helpers?

Of course she does, Chelsea thought. *She didn't even let me handle snacks for the meeting. She had to bring them herself!*

Bang! Chelsea finally shut the door. A little too hard.

Valerie and Gaby both jumped. Good. That meant Chelsea had their full attention. "I have an idea, too," she announced. "I thought we could do a singdown. And we could use the big fireplace to make s'mores." She flipped open Gaby's stupid orange folder and stabbed her finger at the fireplace on the map. "It would be like everybody at the Home was at camp for the night. Nothing could be more fun. Am I right?"

Gaby frowned. "I already did all this work on the scavenger hunt."

"But we haven't decided that's what we're doing," Chelsea protested.

"It's the perfect idea, though," Gaby shot back. "As soon as I came up with it, I knew it was what we had to do."

"Maybe you should have e-mailed us before you did the map and everything," Valerie suggested.

"Volunteering at Home Away From Home was my idea!" Gaby exclaimed.

"So? That doesn't mean you get to decide every-thing. We're volunteering, too," Chelsea snapped.

"Why don't we just try to come up with a bunch of ideas?" Valerie suggested. "That's what today was supposed to be for, right?"

"We don't need a bunch of ideas—" Chelsea began.

"Because mine is the best!" she and Gaby said at the same time, glaring at each other.

Chelsea wanted to be nice. She really did. But it was just so hard around Gaby.

"You know what? I'm out of here," Gaby announced. "There's no way we'd be able to come up with a better idea than the scavenger hunt. That big house could have been built for it. I can't believe you're too stupid to realize that."

Bang! Gaby slammed out the door.

Chelsea and Valerie stared at each other. "I have a whole bunch of snacks in the kitchen," Chelsea finally said. "Do you want to go in there? I could tell you all the details of my Night at Camp plan."

"I don't think it was right for Gaby to plan everything herself," Valerie began.

"I know! Can you believe her?" Chelsea exclaimed.

"But it seems like you did almost the same thing," Valerie reminded her.

"Not true. I didn't make folders!" Chelsea cried.

Valerie let out a sigh and pulled out her cell. "I'm calling my mom. I'm going home. If the three of us are running the activity night together, we should plan it together. That's obviously not happening today." She stepped outside and quietly closed the door behind her.

Great, Chelsea thought. *I spent hours making those snack trays, and no one even got to see them.*

Posted by: Chelsea
Subject: Niceness

I thought all of you might be interested to know how Gaby's decision to become a nicer person is working out.

IT'S NOT. AT ALL.

Supposedly she wanted to volunteer at Home Away From Home because she wanted to be saintly. Actually, she just volunteered so she'd have people to boss around. By people I mean me and Valerie, who she convinced to volunteer with her.

See, Gaby thinks that just because it was her idea to volunteer, she should be in charge. She thinks she should get to decide what we should do at Home Away From Home. I came up with the coolest idea for the activity night that we signed up to run. And Gaby wouldn't even listen. She just didn't think it was possible for anyone else to come up with something cool. She actually stomped out of our planning meeting because she didn't want to hear my suggestions.

Val left, too. And Valerie's usually really nice. So look out everyone—I think Gaby's UN-niceness is catching.

chapter

FIVE

Candace took a tiny bite of her cheese-burger and managed to swallow it. The burgers in the cafeteria really stunk. And her stomach was upset. Again.

You have to eat something, she told herself. *You can't perform the way you should if you're running on empty.* The voice in her head sounded almost exactly like her mother's.

Candace forced down another bite of the burger. Maybe if she was able to finish half of it, she'd be ready to attack those last two math problems again. This was her last chance to get them done. Mr. Merrill always collected homework first thing.

"Hey, Candace, did Ms. Luttinger give a quiz in history?" Samantha asked.

Joshua jumped in before Candace could answer. "She's not telling, and neither am I," he told Samantha. "Why should you get an advantage just because you have history after lunch? We didn't get advance warning—if there was a quiz, which I'm not saying there was. Why should you?"

"Statistically, it's twenty-two percent more likely that we'll get a quiz on Friday than on any other day of the week," Allen said. "My theory is that by Friday, teachers are tired of teaching and just want to sit at their desks and monitor us."

"Yeah, they just want to sit at their desks and monitor us," Candace repeated. Why couldn't she stop doing that? Why?

The real question was why hadn't she just asked for help with her math homework last night? Why?

Her parents or Max would have been happy to help her. Although her dad would have insisted they sharpen all her pencils first. He had this thing about dull pencils. He insisted you couldn't do math unless you had a nice sharp pencil point.

Max might have even turned the homework problems into a game. He did that sometimes, if he didn't have too much homework of his own.

The thing was, if she'd asked anybody in her family for help, it would have meant admitting she was already having trouble in math. And that would have been a big deal. There would have been a huge discussion about what should be done with the Candace-slash-math situation.

Her stomach tensed up just thinking about it. Candace covered her cheeseburger with her napkin. She couldn't stand to look at it anymore. Forget about eating it.

Brynn bounced up and down on her toes. She

felt like she'd drunk two massive bottles of Pepsi. Or like somehow she'd been plugged into an electrical outlet overnight and gotten supercharged. It was always like this before she went onstage: insanely awesome!

"You guys ready?" Drew whispered. "We've got a full house."

Yep. Nearly every seat in the caf was taken. Of course, the kids in those seats were there to eat, not to watch the skit. They didn't even know a performance was about to begin.

"Ready, Freddy," Rosemary answered.

"I'm so ready," Brynn said.

"Then let's do this thang!" Drew raced toward the front of the room, Rosemary and Brynn on his heels. They leaped up onto the stage, not bothering with the three stairs.

"Hello, Wilton Academy!" Rosemary called. "Today Drama League has a special presentation for you."

"Please enjoy this lunchtime performance of *The Dramatics*!" Brynn cried.

There wasn't any applause. No cheers. But Brynn figured that everyone was just waiting to see what happened next.

Drew strode across the stage and mimed opening a refrigerator door. "We're out of milk," he gasped.

Rosemary let out a high, piercing scream. "Noooo!" she screeched. "I bought some at the store yesterday!"

Drew rummaged around in the imaginary fridge. "Well, there's none in here now."

My turn, Brynn thought. She sucked in a deep breath and began to sob. She got actual tears flowing and everything. "I'm sooorrrry," she wailed. "I spilled the milk!"

"What?" Drew roared. "I can't believe this. I can-*not* believe this!" His hands curled into fists and his face turned red. Brynn had never known anyone who could make their cheeks go beet red on command like that. It was truly impressive.

Brynn upped the volume on her sobs. Then Rosemary started to laugh, big, loud hee-haws. "You're crying over spilled milk!" Rosemary told Brynn.

Now it was Brynn's turn to get angry and throw a tantrum because Rosemary had laughed at her. Then Rosemary would start crying. Which would make Drew laugh. Then Brynn and Rosemary would yell at him until he cried. It was important to keep the skit moving fast, fast, fast. It only worked if every few seconds at least one of them switched emotions.

The skit ended with Brynn, Drew, and Rosemary all happy and laughing. Brynn broke out her best high-pitched giggle. It was so loud that at first she didn't realize that no one but the three of them was laughing. *Everyone* in the audience should be laughing by now. This was the big finish!

Drew stepped forward. "Thank you! Thank you!" he called. Even though almost no one was applauding. "We loved putting on this show for you. And we want you to know that there's lots of room in Drama League. So head on over to our table and sign up!"

"All the geeks are already in the club," Joshua,

that friend of Candace's, shouted back. "There are none left to sign up."

That got a laugh from the lunch crowd.

The smile didn't slide off Drew's face. He kept on going with the speech they'd come up with, as if he hadn't even heard what Joshua said. "Join the League and next time it could be you up here."

"Like that's a good thing," somebody muttered.

Brynn gave a bow—just the way she and the others had rehearsed. She kept the smile on her face, too, even though she felt like crying for real. She walked to the edge of the stage and took the three steps down. She didn't feel like she could jump. All the bounce had been sucked out of her legs. She needed to be plugged back into the outlet ASAP. Brynn was almost out of juice.

She couldn't believe it. They'd bombed. They'd totally bombed!

"You were great, Brynn!"

Brynn turned toward the voice, disbelieving, and saw Candace smiling at her. "Thanks, Candace," Brynn said. "Seems like you're the only person who thought so."

She couldn't believe she'd actually thought that joining Drama League was the way to deal with being a new girl. Okay, she had a few friends. But the rest of the people at school thought she was a geek. A geek! And being a geek girl was a lot worse than being a new girl.

"That's not true," Candace protested. Protested weakly, Brynn noted. "It's just that pretty much everyone who goes here is so into academics that they don't really pay attention to anything else." She hesitated. "Maybe it would be good if you joined the debate club. Joshua suggested that, remember?"

What Brynn really remembered was Joshua shouting out the G-word. "I don't know . . . It's not really my thing," she answered.

"It's kind of like drama," Candace said. "But it's cooler."

"So nobody calls kids in the debate club geeks?" Brynn asked.

"Definitely not," Candace told her.

Brynn shook her head. "I'm staying in drama. Acting is my life—even though it wasn't too much fun today."

"I get that," Candace said. "Um, Brynn . . ."

Brynn thought Candace was going to make one more attempt to convince her that she'd be better off in debate. Instead Candace said, "I was up until one o'clock last night, doing research for history. I only got partway thought the math homework, then I fell asleep. Do you think . . ." Candace swallowed hard. "Would it be okay if I copied the last two problems from you?"

Brynn blinked at her in surprise. *But that's cheating,* she thought.

But Candace was her friend. And besides, it was no biggie. Candace had done most of the problems. And they did give a mountain of homework at this school. She'd barely gotten through last night's problems herself.

And, truth, it felt good standing here talking to one of the most popular girls at Wilton. Brynn didn't want to give that up.

"Sure," she told Candace. "Here's my math notebook."

▲ ▲ ▲

When Valerie logged on to the camp blog, Gaby and Chelsea both had a couple of new messages posted. Uh-oh. For a minute she wanted to leap to one of her other favorite sites and just ignore whatever it was Gaby and Chelsea had to say.

But Val didn't have feathers. She wasn't an overgrown chicken. She clicked on Gaby's message. She figured it was Gaby's response to that not-so-nice message about the Home Away From Home planning meeting that ended before it really got started.

Posted by: Gaby
Subject: UN-niceness

You want to know what UN-niceness is? Posting a nasty message about people who are supposed to be your friends.

Posted by: Chelsea
Subject: The Truth Hurts

The message wasn't nasty. It was a simple account of what happened at our so-called planning meeting.

Here's what happened at our so-called planning meeting—just a simple account. I arrived at Chelsea's house. I brought homemade cookies. When Chelsea looked at them she got this expression on her face like she'd just smelled a noxious fart.

I had made up folders for me, Chelsea, and Valerie with my idea for a scavenger hunt. It had hand-drawn maps of the Home Away From Home center with a list of possible hunt items. It had taken me hours of work.

When I showed Chelsea the folder, she threw a total hissy. She slammed the door like she was a three-year-old throwing a tantrum. I expected her to get down on the floor and start kicking her legs. She probably did after I left.

Valerie wasn't much better. She got all snotty and said maybe I should have e-mailed and gotten her per-mission before I put in all my hours of work. Which I did because I want the activity night to be awesome for the brothers and sisters of the kids who are dying!

"I did not get all snotty," Valerie told the computer screen. Her fingers itched to shoot off an answer—one that showed exactly what snotty really sounded like. But that would be like, "Gasoline, I'd like you to meet fire." No. She would leave the blog war to Chelsea and Gaby.

Valerie decided not to even read the rest of the Chelsea and Gaby messages. She was almost sure they'd just make her crazy angry. She moved on to a post by Brynn instead.

I have a question for all of you. How would you define a geek? This is ultra-important, so please answer, okay? And soon, please.

▲ ▲ ▲

So somebody basically called me a geek today, Brynn thought. *So what. They called Rosemary and Drew geeks, too. And they aren't. Which means I'm not.*

"Aaargh!" she groaned. She hated that she cared about the geek incident. But she did.

Brynn checked the clock. It had only been fifteen minutes since she'd posted her question about what exactly made someone a geek. But maybe somebody had answered. She logged on to the camp blog. There were a ton of responses!

Posted by: Chelsea
Subject: Geekiness

Anyone who needs a definition for geek is, by definition, a geek.

Yowch, Brynn thought. But that was Chelsea. The girl could be really harsh. Brynn decided to ignore her—or at least try to ignore her. She went on to the next message.

Posted by: Natalie
Subject: Geekiness

In the movies, geeks are actually the interesting kids. They're the artists. The rebels. The guys who look really cute with floppy hair and glasses. The girls with the funky clothes. If I could walk into the world of some of my fave movies, I'd definitely want to hang with the geeks.

Posted by: Grace
Subject: Geekiness

Um, I think I am, or at least have been in the past, a geek. Remember all those teddy bears I brought to camp the first year? Some of you thought I was a geek then. Didn't you? Didn't you? It's okay. I thought some of you were geeks, too. And I liked you anyway.

Posted by: Priya
Subject: Geekiness

I have no idea.

Posted by: Alex
Subject: Geekiness

Dictionary definition: a person often of an intellectual bent who is disliked.

Posted by: Gaby
Subject: Geekiness

I hate to agree with Chelsea. But I agree with Chelsea.

Posted by: Alyssa
Subject: Geekiness

I'm a proud art geek. And, Brynn, I'm doing a painting for your new bedroom. The painting won't be geeky.

Posted by: Jenna
Subject: Geekiness

I was watching *Beauty and the Geek*, and a bunch of guys thought the only definition of "booty" was pirate treasure. That says it all, right?

Brynn got an IM before she could read the next answer. She clicked on the pop-up window to read it. It was from Alex.

<SoccerLover>: What's up, B? What's the real deal on the geek question?
<BrynnWins>: Somebody basically called me a geek today. Can you see my salty tears through your monitor?
<SoccerLover>: Who should I beat up? Just give me a name.
<BrynnWins>: LOL. Let me give you a list of pretty much everyone at my school. To them, if you're in drama, you're a geek. I'm thinking of switching from Drama League to the debate team.
<SoccerLover>: No. If you do, I'll have to beat you up,

too. That's like saying you're thinking of not being Brynn anymore. You have to stay in drama.

Brynn hesitated, staring at Alex's IM. She looked around her room, taking in the paper flowers she'd carried when she was Eliza in *My Fair Lady*, the green hat she'd worn when she was Peter Pan at camp, the pictures of the entire cast of *Hansel and Gretel*, the first play Brynn was ever in.

Her computer gave a ding and another IM came up.

<[Grrrrace]>: Alex just IM'd me that you're thinking of giving up drama. You can't do it. I know how much you love it. I'd die if I couldn't act, and I know you would, too. You have to promise me that you'll stay in the club. PROMISE!

Brynn smiled as she typed her answer.

<BrynnWins>: I promise!!!

chapter
SIX

"I knew I'd get an A," Max said. He paused to shovel a spoonful of mashed potatoes into his mouth. Then started talking again before he'd barely chewed. "But I didn't think I'd get a hundred percent. There was this one question I thought I'd messed up on."

"Great work," Candace's dad told him.

"Great work," Candace echoed, wondering why neither of her parents bothered to mention Max's not-so-great table manners.

"Oh, and I'm going to head up a team for science fair. People were practically killing one another to get on my team," Max continued. He stuffed an entire stalk of asparagus into his mouth. "Everybody was really psyched about my engine-run-by-decomposing-garbage idea."

"You take the team to victory, and that'll make a nice addition to your college apps," Candace's dad commented.

"Oh, we're going to win," Max answered with a grin. "I worked all summer on coming up with the experiments."

What did I do all summer? Candace thought.

Then she remembered. Camp. She wished she was back there right now!

"How did the first week of school treat you, Candy?" her mother asked, using Candace's little-girl nickname.

"Good," Candace said. "We had a quiz in history today. Supposedly more teachers give quizzes on Fridays, at least according to Allen."

"That guy has a statistic for everything," Max commented. "I've only met him a couple of times, and I think he got out about fifteen statistics per conversation."

"Yeah, he likes the statistics," Candace agreed.

"How do you think you did on the quiz?" her dad asked.

"We exchanged papers and graded them in class. I got a perfect score," Candace answered, happy to have something good to report.

"Great, sweetie," her mom said. "And how's math so far? Do you like your new teacher?"

"Mr. Merrill is great!" Candace answered enthusiastically. "I like him a lot." Which was true. Mr. Merrill was really patient when she didn't understand something. She bet he'd explain things twenty more times if she needed him to. She was just too embarrassed to admit that that's exactly what she did need.

"So shall we just hold off on a tutor for a while, then?" her dad asked her.

Candace hesitated. Part of her wanted to say no, please get me a tutor STAT. A big part. But the part that wanted to say yes was a little bigger. She needed help. She knew she needed help. Still, Candace just wasn't ready to have all her parents' attention focused on her. All that worry.

"I think I'm good," she answered. "Algebra is different than other kinds of math. People who aren't that great at math can be algebra stars." It was something that Mr. Merrill had said the first day of class.

"It's true," Max agreed. And for once Candace wasn't grossed out that he was talking with his mouth full. "You think in a different way when you do algebra than you do in the math you learn before that."

"Now that we've gotten the school report, let's talk about next weekend," Candace's mom suggested. "I'm thinking it's time for one of our family outings."

"Can't," Max said. "I'm going camping with the Finns, remember?"

"Oh, that's right. Time goes by so quickly. I can't believe it's time for the camping trip already," Candace's mom answered. She smiled at Candace. "What do you think of having a party that weekend, with your big brother out of the picture? A party is always a great way to kick off the new school year. There are tons of your friends that you've hardly seen over the summer."

I don't deserve a party, Candace thought. *Not after all that lying. If my parents knew the truth about how I'm doing in math, they'd be pulling together a list of tutors right now.*

But if she told them the truth, in less than an hour she would have her weekend plans. Math, math, and more math.

Candace took a sip of water. Her mouth and

throat had turned to dry sandpaper. "A party sounds great," she finally said.

▲ ▲ ▲

Brynn checked the audition schedule. She'd be the third girl up. That was a decent slot. It was better to go near the beginning or the end. At the beginning, the people you were auditioning for were fresh. They were eager to find the best person for each part. They hadn't heard the same song one billion times. At the end, if you really rocked, the people you were auditioning for remembered you, because they didn't have to watch a billion other actors after you.

Not that there were anywhere near a billion actors auditioning for the Wilton Academy production of *Little Shop of Horrors*. There weren't anywhere near a *hundred*. The number of girls auditioning for Audrey, the lead, was less than ten. Brynn had never been to an audition with so few people to compete against. It kind of made the whole process less fun. Definitely less of a challenge.

I have a good shot at playing Audrey, Brynn thought. It was an amazing part. Tons of good songs. Lots of time onstage. You got a chance to be funny, but you also got a chance to tug at the audience's heartstrings, too.

So why don't I feel more excited? she asked herself.

Duh, she thought. *Maybe because starring in the school play pretty much equals social suicide. At least at this freaky school.*

Mr. Saunders, the director, called Brynn's name. It was already her turn. Brynn forced a smile on her face and bounded up to the stage. She might not be feeling completely sure that she wanted to be in this play, but she wasn't going to let Mr. Saunders or anybody else get even a whiff of doubt from her.

She handed the girl sitting at the piano the sheet music for "Part of Your World," the song from *The Little Mermaid* where Ariel sings her soul out about wanting to be in the human world.

Brynn had chosen "Part of Your World" because it expressed the same emotions as Audrey's big song, "Somewhere That's Green," and was even written by the same guys who were the lyricist and composer for *Little Shop*. But "Part of Your World" was a song that Mr. Saunders wouldn't have heard a hundred—okay, ten—girls sing by the time auditions were over.

As soon as she got out the first line, Brynn was Ariel. She wasn't thinking about popularity. She wasn't thinking about wanting to get cast in the play. She was just thinking about wanting to experience the world above the ocean, where the humans lived.

She was oblivious to anything else until the music stopped. Then she was suddenly aware of another sound. The sound of snickering from the back of the room. Her face flushed as she realized that several people—popular-type people—were watching the auditions.

They looked like they thought her song had been the funniest song they'd ever heard. And "Part of Your World"? It was about longing. It was about wishing for another life. How could they think that was funny? What was wrong with them?

Or was it Brynn who had something wrong with her?

▲ ▲ ▲

I can't just go up to her and ask if I can copy her math homework. Especially not after I already did it once, Candace thought. She stood at the end of the hall, watching Brynn pull books out of her locker on Tuesday.

But the thing was, she couldn't turn in her math homework partially done, either. And Brynn wasn't like her other friends, or her parents, or Max. She wouldn't be all judgmental. She wouldn't think Candace was some kind of loser.

Candace took a step down the hall, toward Brynn. Then hesitated. It was true that Brynn wouldn't think Candace was a loser because she was having trouble with math. But that didn't mean that she'd be okay with cheating. Because that's what Candace would be asking her to do. Cheat.

"Hi, Candace!"

Brynn's voice jerked Candace away from her thoughts. Brynn was about two feet away. Candace hadn't even noticed Brynn walk away from her locker. "Um, hi," she answered.

Brynn started past her. "Wait!" Candace cried.

"What's up?" Brynn asked.

"I need . . ." Candace couldn't get the request for math homework out of her mouth. "I need to ask you to come to a party I'm having this weekend," she said in a rush.

"Really?" Brynn replied. "That sounds fun."

"It sounds fun, right?" Candace echoed. "It's on Saturday, starting at seven thirty, at my house. You have the address on the camp contact sheet, right?" Candace asked. Even though she and Brynn had both always lived in the Boston area, they'd never been to each other's houses.

"Yup. I'll be there. Thanks!" Brynn said. And she started to walk away.

"Wait!" Candace blurted.

Brynn paused.

Candace tried to think of what to say. How could she ask for the homework? "Uh, I just wanted to say that you can bring someone if you want to. To the party."

"Cool. That would be great," Brynn said.

Now ask her about the homework, Candace ordered herself. *Ask her or she's going to walk away and you can't stop her again.*

"It's going to be really fun," Candace said. Hadn't she already kind of said that? Didn't matter. She pushed on. "I was up so late making plans. What to eat and everything. I . . . I didn't get my math homework done. Again." Her heart started fluttering, beating faster than a hummingbird's wings. "Would you mind if I borrowed yours?"

Brynn hesitated for a second.

Please, please, please, Candace thought. She couldn't go into math without that homework. She just couldn't.

"Oh, why not?" Brynn said. "It will be my contribution to a fabulous party." She pulled her backpack off her shoulder, unzipped it, and pulled out her math notebook.

Shame flooded Candace as she reached out for it. But she took the notebook anyway. She had no choice.

Valerie stood on the walkway leading to the Home Away From Home house. *Get in there,* she told herself.

But she didn't want to.

It should be fun, she figured. It was movie night at the Home. Val, Chelsea, and Gaby were observing to prep for the activity night they were going to run. And observing movie night—that was pretty much just watching a movie. Val loved movies. So, fun, right?

Definitely fun. Except for two things. Chelsea and Gaby.

Valerie didn't know what to expect from her teammates. Would they be able to get through movie night without screaming, or hair pulling, or bloodshed? All Val knew for sure was that she didn't want to get between them. And that meant she didn't want to go inside Home Away From Home.

"Are you suffering from some kind of malfunction?" a voice asked from behind her. "Why are you just standing there?"

Valerie didn't have to turn around to identify the speaker.

Party time, she thought. "Hey, Gabs. I was just thinking."

"And you hurt yourself?" Gaby joked as they walked toward the house together.

Oh, yeah. It is party time. Woo-hoo, Valerie thought. "I don't think I strained my brain," she answered, trying to keep the irritation out of her voice. "I was wondering how it would go tonight," she admitted. Why not just be honest? "I've been reading the posts going back and forth between you and Chelsea, and I thought maybe I needed a black-and-white striped shirt and a whistle for tonight."

Gaby looked at her blankly.

"You know . . . like a referee," Valerie explained.

"You'd need a lot more than a shirt and a whistle to keep Chelsea in line," Gaby answered. "Can you believe what she said about us in those posts?"

Us. Had Gaby forgotten that she called Val snotty in one of her messages? Valerie decided to let it go. That and Chelsea calling Valerie un-nice. The last thing they needed tonight was more mess.

She pulled open the front door and stepped inside. "You're here! Finally," Chelsea said. "Ms. Jeunet was wondering where you were."

Gaby's eyebrows shot up. "You were talking to Ms. Jeunet?" she cried.

"She introduced me to the frat guys who are running movie night," Chelsea answered. "Too bad you missed it." She grinned. "They were all really cute. And they were really impressed that I'm volunteering here."

"Did you tell them it was my idea?" Gaby demanded.

"You weren't here," Chelsea answered with a shrug.

Valerie could see the muscles in Gaby's jaw tighten. *Duck and cover*, she thought.

But before Gaby could blow, Ms. Jeunet hurried up. "Girls, you're here," she said to Val and Gaby. "Chelsea wasn't sure you would be." She rushed on before either of them could protest. "The guys are about to get the movie started, but I thought we could grab a few minutes to touch base about what you have planned for your activity night. Chelsea started to say something about an event with singing, but I was called away on a popcorn crisis before I heard all the details."

"Right," Chelsea answered quickly. "We wanted to do a singdown. What you do is—"

"You come up with teams, and you give each team a list of items to search for in the house," Gaby interrupted.

Ms. Jeunet's brow furrowed. "I'm not sure where the singing comes in," she said.

"That's because there is no singing—" Gaby began.

"During the scavenger hunt part of the night," Valerie said, thinking fast. "We have three activities planned. A scavenger hunt, a singdown, and uh, um, a round of charades. We'll have teams for the night, and everyone on the team that wins the most events gets a prize. Plus the losers will get consolation prizes," she finished up, breathless.

"That sounds great! I love the idea of teams. That's a great way for the kids to get to know one another. There are always new families coming to the Home, so there are always new kids who haven't met many people." Ms. Jeunet smiled. "I can't wait. But now I have to dash. The DVD player is a little temperamental. I want to make sure the boys aren't having any problems." She started toward the living room. "Manny!" she called to a shaggy-haired boy sitting on the stairs. "Come with me. I might need your technical expertise."

As soon as Ms. Jeunet and Manny were out of sight, Chelsea and Gaby both whirled to face Valerie. "Why did you do that? That's not what we planned," Chelsea whisper-yelled.

"We didn't plan anything," Valerie reminded her. "Not anything we all agreed on, anyway."

"I still say my idea is best," Gaby said. "And I already did so much work on the scav—"

"I. Don't. Care," Valerie announced. "Ms. Jeunet already said she loved the idea of three activities. That's what we're doing. Unless one of you wants to go tell her that the three of us have been fighting for days because we can't agree on what we want to do with the kids who have brothers and sisters who are really sick!"

"Fine," Gaby snapped. "But I'm finishing planning the scavenger hunt by myself. I don't need your help. Or want it."

"Works for me," Chelsea answered. "I'll do the singdown on my own. It's going to be the best activity of the night."

"I guess that means I'll handle the charades solo," Valerie said. "Wow. I'm so glad we're doing this volunteering thing together!" She turned on her heel and walked into the living room. She didn't care if Gaby or Chelsea followed her. Right now, she didn't care if she never saw either of them again.

▲ ▲ ▲

Gaby stared at the TV screen, but she couldn't make herself pay attention to the movie. All she could think about was how out of control the volunteering situation had gotten. The whole thing was her idea, and now she was only in charge of one little part of the activity night. Thanks to Valerie. Gaby couldn't believe Val had taken over like that.

A bolt of pain zigzagged through Gaby's foot, making her forget everything else—even the horrible Val and Chelsea. "Watch it!" she hissed at the boy who'd just stomped on her as he headed out of the room.

He just scowled at her and kept on going. Talk about un-nice. What was his problem?

Suddenly Gaby remembered where she was— Home Away From Home. And she got what the boy's problem was. Somebody in his family was seriously ill. The movie night was supposed to be taking his mind off all the bad stuff in his life. And clearly it wasn't working.

So the nice thing to do (and the whole point of being here was to be a nicer person) would be to go after him. Talk to him. Try to, to . . . comfort him. Gaby smiled. She was doing it.

She stood up, leaving Chelsea and Valerie behind to watch the movie. Like they were just here to enjoy themselves. She checked the kitchen, the dining room, and the office before she found the boy in the small library.

"What do you want?" the boy snapped. He was about Gaby's age, maybe a year older, with longish sandy hair that flopped into his eyes.

"I want an apology. You stepped on my foot before," Gaby shot back, before she remembered she was on a Mission of Mercy. She liked the sound of that. Mission of Mercy. "Just kidding," Gaby added quickly. "I actually came to find you because I thought you could use somebody to talk to."

The boy snorted.

It isn't nice to snort when somebody is trying to be nice to you, Gaby thought. "What's your name, anyway?" she asked.

"Leland. Now you probably want to know how I'm feeling," he answered.

She'd already broken through to him. She was good at this. "I do want to know how you're feeling," Gaby told him. "I really do. I know you're going through a hard—"

"You don't know anything about me," Leland interrupted. "And you know what else? You don't care."

"I do too," Gaby protested.

"Uh-uh. I've been coming to places like this for years. I've seen your type before," Leland said, shoving his hair out of his eyes. "You care like crazy what people think of you, and you're here so everyone will think you're such a sweet girl."

"That's not true!" Gaby cried. Even though he'd so nailed it. It was like her head was made of clear plastic and he could read her deepest, most secret thoughts. She'd wanted Ms. Jeunet to think she was a good person. Ms. Jeunet and everyone at the center, and her parents, and every friend she'd told about her volunteer work.

"Get lost," Leland said. He grabbed a book off the nearest shelf. "I came in here to be alone. Not to help you score brownie points."

"I'm here to help," Gaby yelled. "You could be a little grateful. You're the most inconsiderate person I've ever met!"

"If you leave you won't have to be around me anymore," Leland answered. He didn't look up from his book. Like he was all involved in *Are You There God? It's Me, Margaret*. Yeah, right.

"Don't worry about it. I'm gone. You don't deserve anybody being nice to you." Gaby stormed out of the library and slammed the door behind her. Then she leaned against it, legs trembling.

She was horrible. She was completely, thoroughly horrible. She had to be the worst volunteer ever. She had actually just screamed at one of the kids she was supposed to be trying to make feel better.

Maybe I'm the kind of person who just can't be nice, Gaby thought, tears stinging her eyes. *Maybe I just don't have it in me. Maybe I really am just a bad person.*

▲ ▲ ▲

"Hey, sugar cookie. How did it go tonight?"

Chelsea's dad asked when she came home from the movie night.

"Great!" Chelsea answered. "But my camp night is going to be even better. I'm going to have everyone make s'mores in the fireplace, and we're going to have a singdown. That's when you divide everyone into teams, then you call out a word, and the teams have to sing a song with that word in it. You just keep going from team to team to team, until a team can't come up with another song. Then they're out."

"Sounds fun." Her father took a long pull on his water bottle.

"It's going to be perfection!" Chelsea answered. "Oooh! And I just thought of a way to make it perfection plus. Nametags! I'm going to make beautiful nametags for everyone."

"Sounds fun," her father repeated. His voice sounded a little flat, and Chelsea suddenly realized how tired he looked.

She flashed on an image of him during the worst of his chemo. He'd come home and go straight to bed, and he'd looked like . . . like he was partway dead.

"Long day?" she asked, trying to sound casual.

"Yeah. Your old man went to the gym after work. I know exercise is supposed to make you feel good, but I'm still at the stage where it makes me want to crawl straight into bed."

Chelsea laughed, relief whooshing through her. He was looking bad because he was getting healthy!

"Poor dad," she said.

"Poor old dad," he agreed with a smile.

"I'm going to head to my room. I want to get started right away designing those nametags," Chelsea told him.

Her father gave her a hug. "I'm so proud of you for doing this."

"Thanks, Dad!" Chelsea answered. It felt so good hearing him say that. Having him around to be able to say that.

"My part of the activity night is going to be way more fabulous than Gaby and Valerie's," she promised him when he let her go. "I'm going to make sure all those kids who have sick people in their families have an awesome time!"

chapter
EIGHT

"Good morning, students. Today is Friday and this morning's word is *agrestic*. Agrestic is defined as pertaining to fields or the country; rural; rustic."

Brynn glanced around her homeroom as the morning announcements sounded over the PA system. Lots of people were writing down the word and its definition. She sighed. Would she ever get used to the constant stream of academics at this school? It was exhausting to feel like you should be learning something every single second of the day.

". . . happy to announce the cast list for this fall's Drama League production of *Little Shop of Horrors*," the voice went on.

Brynn sat up straight. Now this was more like it!

"Playing the part of Seymour will be Drew Brody . . ."

Yay, Drew! Brynn thought. Her friend had landed the male lead, and she knew he would be perfect for the part.

"And in the role of Audrey, we have Brynn Collins."

Brynn felt her cheeks flush with pleasure. "Yes!" she cried, pumping her fist in the air. She'd done it! She'd gotten the lead role! She looked around the room, wanting to share her happiness, wanting to receive some congratulations. That was how it had always worked at her old school.

But the other kids in her homeroom just stared at her like she was crazy.

"Yes! I'm a total geek!" somebody muttered. A couple of other kids laughed.

Embarrassed, Brynn lowered her hand.

"Wow, Brynn, it's nice to have a big star in our room," the teacher said politely. "Congratulations."

"Thanks," Brynn murmured. She looked back down at her desk, where she'd been doodling pictures of Audrey II, the man-eating plant from the play. She couldn't wait until homeroom was over so she could find her drama friends. At least *they* would be psyched about the play.

Just as she'd expected, Drew was waiting for her outside homeroom with a huge, excited grin on his face. "You got it!" he cried.

"*You* got it!" Brynn replied, laughing. They slapped a high five. "I can't wait to start rehearsals," she went on. "That's one of my favorite things in the world, rehearsing for a play. I just love to see it all start to come together."

"Me too." Drew headed down the hallway, and Brynn followed. "It's so much fun to spend all that time in the auditorium after school. I spend all day looking forward to it."

"How long are we going to rehearse?" Brynn asked. "At my old school we had two months."

"Not that long," Drew replied. "The play goes up in six weeks."

"Wow, that sounds so soon." Brynn felt a little thrill of anticipation. She could hardly wait to be up onstage again—the hot lights in her face, the energy of the crowd charging her performance . . .

"Do you think Candace will come see the show?" Drew asked, fake-casually. "I mean, since you guys are buds and everything?"

Brynn stopped walking and turned to Drew. As usual when he was talking about Candace, the tips of his ears were red. She smiled. "You know what? I'm going to do you a big favor," she told him.

"Huh?" he asked.

"Candace is having a party tomorrow night, a big back-to-school thing," Brynn said. "She invited me, and I can bring a guest. So I'm going to bring you."

"Me?" Drew's voice squeaked, but he seemed too excited to notice. "Really?"

"Really. That way instead of just asking me about Candace, you can actually talk to her yourself," Brynn said. "Since you obviously like her."

"What? I do not," Drew answered quickly.

Brynn just raised her eyebrows.

"Oh, fine, I do," he mumbled. "I like her."

"I knew it!" Brynn cried. "You're so obvious about it. It's really cute."

"You make me sound like a puppy," Drew complained. "It's not cute. It stinks. I've had a huge crush on her since last year and I've never even said more than two words to her. I'm such a loser."

"You are not, you're just embarrassed," Brynn told him as they started walking again.

"I know. I can get up onstage and act in front of tons of people and not feel embarrassed at all," Drew said. "But the second I see Candace, I get all nervous."

"Once you talk to her, you'll stop feeling nervous," Brynn promised. "And that's why this party is the perfect idea. You'll come with me, you'll have to talk to Candace because she's the hostess, and then you'll get over your nervousness. Plus, you'll have a chance to actually get to know her instead of just hearing about her from other people."

"Yeah." A slow smile made its way across Drew's face. "Yeah, you're right. Thanks, Brynn!"

"No problem." Brynn turned toward her science classroom. "See you later."

"Later!"

As Drew headed off in the other direction, Brynn smiled to herself. It felt good to do something nice for him. Now she had a reason to look forward to the party—she'd been a little worried about going to a place filled with all the popular, academic kids. Who knew if she'd find anyone to talk to? But with Drew there, she had an instant posse.

And besides, it will be good for Candace, she thought. She had seemed seriously stressed the few times Brynn had talked to her. Candace had never been the life of the party at camp, but she'd always been up for having fun. Here at school, though, she was like a completely different person. Brynn had barely even seen her smile.

Candace needs to have some fun so she can relax, Brynn thought. *And Drew is fun.*

It was the perfect plan!

To: imnotmichaelJORDAN@rcn.com
From: Brynnwins@pc.com
Subject: I got it!

I got the part! I'm Audrey in Little Shop of Horrors! I'm so excited! And not only that, in addition to my flourishing acting career, I've also taken up a little matchmaking on the side. Pretty exciting stuff. I guess you could say things are looking up! Phew . . . I feel so much better.

Just wanted to share. Talk soon—
XO-Brynn

I wish it was August again, Candace thought on Saturday afternoon. *Then I could be lying by the lake or hiking in the woods instead of doing stupid math homework.*

She stared down at her notebook. The quadratic equation. Twenty problems, all to be solved using the quadratic equation. Candace sighed. This was supposed to be easy. She just had to plug the numbers into the equation and solve it, the same way every time. But somehow it didn't work out. No matter what she did, something always went wrong.

Max would have no trouble with this, she thought, frustrated. *He'd have solved every problem on this page and be on to his science homework by now.*

It just wasn't fair. How come her brother was so good at math when she was so bad? Shouldn't there be a family math gene or something? He'd never gotten anything less than an A in math. She should be the same way.

"How's it coming, sweetie?" her mother asked, leaning in the doorway of Candace's room.

"Great!" Candace chirped, pasting a big smile on her face. "I'm almost done."

Her mom smiled back. "That's wonderful, Candace. I'm so glad math is easier for you this year."

Candace felt a pang of guilt as her mother left. She hated lying to her parents. But she hated disappointing them even more. They were used to having kids who got good grades. She simply had to find a way to deliver.

But the numbers in her notebook seemed to swim in front of her eyes when she looked back down. Her mom had interrupted her in the middle of a problem, and now Candace couldn't even remember what she had been doing.

"This is hopeless," she sighed. She glanced at the clock on her desk. It was almost five o'clock. Her party started at seven thirty. She still had to shower, find a really cool outfit to wear, pick out CDs to play, and get all the snacks and sodas ready.

I might as well start getting ready now, Candace

thought. *I'm obviously not going to get my math done before the party.*

She closed her notebook and trudged toward the bathroom to take a shower. It would be nice if she could look forward to her own party, but she knew it was just going to be a bunch of people talking about schoolwork.

Candace felt her stomach twist into knots just thinking about it.

Was she ever going to have fun again?

▲ ▲ ▲

"Harvard. That's really the only choice," Joshua said three hours later. "It's the best college in the country. Why wouldn't you want to go to the best?"

"It's not the best school for engineering," Rowan argued. "You could go to MIT or . . ."

Candace glanced away, checking the front door to see if there were any new arrivals at the party. She really didn't want to be part of this conversation. She'd expected her friends to talk a lot about school, but she hadn't been expecting them to start talking about college! It was hard enough trying to survive eighth grade.

"What about you, Candace?" Rowan was saying.

"What about me?" Candace asked. She hadn't been paying attention. Could they tell?

"What subject are you going to concentrate in once we get to high school?" Samantha asked.

"Concentrate?" Candace repeated.

"Weren't you even listening?" Samantha teased.

"Rowan read an article that said that colleges want to see a clear major in your academic record from high school. That way they know you're a committed student."

"Oh. Um . . . I don't know yet," Candace admitted. "Do we really have to decide so soon?" The very idea of it made her anxious. She obviously couldn't concentrate in math. English was her best subject. But did she really want to make it the most important thing in her life for the next five years?

"No, I think it's stupid," Joshua said. "My older sister never concentrated in anything and she got into Yale. I bet that article was wrong. I bet as long as you have As in all your classes, the colleges don't care what you concentrate in."

Candace glanced over at the door again—and saw her mom greeting Brynn. She knew she should go over and say hi, too. But now that Brynn was here, it felt kind of weird that Candace had invited her. Brynn just didn't fit in with the rest of the people at the party.

"Excuse me," she told her friends. Then she headed for the door. Brynn had somebody with her, a guy from school. Candace had seen him around, but she didn't know him.

"Hi! Thanks for coming," she said to them.

"Hi, Candace. Thanks for inviting me." Brynn gave her a warm smile. "Do you know my friend Drew?" She gestured to the boy, who was running his hand through his thick dark hair.

"Not really." She held out her hand. "Hi. I've seen you at school."

"You have?" He turned red. "I mean, yeah, I've seen you, too." He shook her hand. "I'm Drew. But Brynn just said that. So you already know it. I'm Drew."

Candace glanced at Brynn. Was this guy being funny or weird? She wasn't sure. Brynn was laughing, though, so he must be being funny. Candace smiled. "You're Drew," she repeated.

"Yeah."

"Drew is in Drama League with me," Brynn told her. "He's going to be the star of *Little Shop of Horrors*."

"Great," Candace said. Not that anyone at the party would think so.

"I'm not the only star. Brynn is also a star," Drew replied. "And really, the big star is the plant."

"The plant?" Candace asked.

"Yeah. It's a giant man-eating plant. So, you know, it's much more interesting than I am." He ran his hand through his hair again.

"A man-eating plant?" Candace said, frowning. "Is there such a thing?"

Drew's eyes widened. "I hope not. I get freaked out just watering my mother's regular old spider plants. I don't even want to think about a plant that might look at me and wonder if I'd go well on a sandwich with some mayonnaise."

Candace laughed, a real laugh that relaxed every muscle in her body. "Spider plants aren't spiders, you know."

"But they look like spiders. Hence the freaking out," Drew replied. "I hate spiders."

"Candace and I once battled a one-inch-long

spider in our cabin at camp," Brynn said. "Remember that thing?"

"Ugh, yes," Candace said. "It was this big brown one with a yellow dot on its back, and it kept *looking* at me—"

"Hello, I hate spiders," Drew interrupted. "Did you guys not hear me? Hate. Spiders."

Brynn and Candace giggled. "Sorry," Brynn said. "No more spider talk."

"Thank you. What should we talk about instead?" Drew asked.

"Anything but school," Candace blurted without thinking. It wasn't something she'd ever have said in front of Joshua or Rowan. But Brynn and Drew just made her feel comfortable. Like she didn't have to carefully choose each word.

"No problem there," Brynn said. "It's a party. Who wants to think about school at a party?"

All of my friends, Candace thought.

"Seriously. It's too stressful to think about school on the weekend. We should be thinking about movies," Drew said. "I went to see that new Keanu one last night. There was at least one explosion every ten minutes. It was incredible."

"I like him better in romantic movies," Candace said.

"Yeah, me too," Drew answered quickly.

Candace stared at him, then burst out laughing.

"What?" he asked.

"No boy likes romantic movies better than action movies," she said.

"That's true. I'm totally lying," Drew agreed. "But I would totally go to a romantic movie with you." Candace noticed the tips of his ears getting red. "Would you want to? Go to a romantic movie? Or even a movie about spiders?"

Brynn knocked shoulders with him. "Smooth," she commented.

Candace couldn't believe Drew had just asked her out. She hardly even knew him.

But she knew enough to know she'd probably spend the whole night laughing. And not talking about school.

"Candace, aren't you going to pull out TriBond? I want a rematch," Joshua called.

"Um, I should . . ." Candace said, taking a step away.

"Wait. You can't leave me hanging," Drew protested. "Tell me no if you must, but I have to have an answer. Otherwise it's cruel and unusual."

"It would be fun . . ."

And it would be, it would be so much fun. But she couldn't do it.

"But I have so much homework. I have time to brush my teeth when I'm done, and that's it. So I can't. Sorry." She rushed away to Joshua, Rowan, and Samantha. "I think the game's up in my brother's room," she told them.

"No rush. We just saw that you needed rescuing," Samantha said.

Candace felt her forehead get wrinkly. "Rescuing?"

"From the drama geeks," Joshua explained with a grin.

"Oh." That's all she said. Oh. She knew she should tell her friends how cool and fun Drew and Brynn were.

But she knew they wouldn't get it.

And she didn't want to get into some big thing with them. She had enough problems in her life already.

▲ ▲ ▲

Brynn coughed, a piece of tortilla chip suddenly refusing to go all the way down her throat. All she'd wanted when she headed over to the end table was a snack. Instead she ended up hearing a whole bunch of nasty about her and Drew.

And Candace hadn't said anything to defend them.

It's so not fair. None of Candace's friends really know Drew or me, Brynn thought. She lifted her chin. They didn't. But they were going to. Brynn wasn't going to run away crying—even though part of her wanted to. She was staying. She was going to work this party. These were the most popular kids at school.

She thought about getting Drew to mingle with her. But she decided they'd have an easier time with the socializing if they stayed apart.

She wandered into the kitchen. Two boys and a girl were chatting near the sodas. Brynn grabbed the bottle of Diet Coke and poured herself a glass. "Hi," she said to the boy nearest to her.

"Hey." He gave her a brief nod.

"I'm Brynn," she said. "I'm new at Wilton."

"Yeah, I know. You're in my music class," he told her. "I'm Scott."

"Oh. Right, hi." Brynn was embarrassed that she hadn't recognized him. "Sorry. I'm bad with faces."

"Don't worry about it, nobody remembers Scott," the girl said, teasing him. She smiled at Brynn. "I'm Marina, and this is Glen."

"It's nice to meet you guys," Brynn said, relaxing a little. These people were being nice. Clearly not everyone thought she was a drama geek unworthy of speaking to.

"So the junior college is offering a theory class over the holiday break," Glen said. "Anyone want to take it with me?"

Marina frowned. "I'm not sure. Won't it be too advanced? If it's actually a college class, I mean."

"Yeah, but you don't have to put it on your transcript if you get a bad grade," Scott said. "And then when you take it again in high school, you'll have an advantage."

"Um, what's a theory class?" Brynn asked, confused.

"Music theory," Scott said. "You know, learning how to write music and stuff like that."

"Oh." She wasn't sure what else to say.

"Are you into music?" Glen asked.

"Of course she is. Why else would she be taking music class with me?" Scott said.

"Actually, I just chose it because Wilton required

an arts class and I figured music went better with my interest in drama than sculpture did," Brynn explained. "I'm really into acting. That's my passion."

"Oh," Marina said.

"That's cool, I guess," Scott said.

"So are you guys up for the theory class or what?" Glen asked. "Registration ends next Friday."

They kept talking, and Brynn kept smiling and pretending to be interested. But there was a hollow feeling in her stomach. Even the nice people here were so into classes and grades.

"See you later," she finally mumbled and headed back into the living room. *If I'm going to do this, I should do it all the way,* she decided. She headed toward Samantha, Joshua, Rowan, and Allen. They were in the middle of a debate about whether or not you got a superior education at boarding school. Were they for real?

Even though she thought the conversation was sort of silly, she wanted to join in. *Too bad the only boarding school I know anything about is Hogwarts,* she thought.

She'd just about stepped up to the group when Samantha glanced over at her, then purposely inched closer to Joshua until there was no room between them. She whispered something to him, he looked at Brynn for a second, and they both laughed.

Brynn kept walking, pretending not to notice. But her heart was pounding hard in her chest. That had been so harsh! *They're all so rude,* Brynn told herself. *You're better off not being friends with them.*

So why did she still want them to like her?

"Suddenly Seymour is standing beside you!" Drew sang, his voice echoing through the empty auditorium.

"He don't give me orders. He don't condescend," Brynn joined in. Her voice blended perfectly with Drew's, and when they finished, everyone in Drama League cheered and whooped. Drew held out his hand for a fist bump.

Grinning, Brynn touched her fist to his.

"This is going to be the best production in the history of Wilton Academy," he said. "It's only the first rehearsal and already we rock."

"You were flat for the entire first verse," their drama advisor said wryly.

"Mr. Saunders, you cannot kill my joy," Drew replied, laughing.

"Okay, I want to work on the choreography for the scene where the dentist meets his end," Mr. Saunders said. "Brynn, you're not in this scene, so you can take a breather. But don't go far—we're going to work on your scenes with the dentist next. James has to miss the next two rehearsals, so I want to make sure we go over all his scenes today."

"Got it." Brynn skipped down the steps from the stage, then headed out to the hall for a drink of water.

She felt like running right back into the auditorium when she saw Samantha walking toward her. *You are so not going to run from that girl,* Brynn ordered herself.

Samantha paused and gave a mocking half curtsy. "All hail the queen of the geeks," she said loudly, then continued on past Brynn.

Brynn sank down on the bench next to the drinking fountain. Her legs had gone to jelly. She didn't think she could stand up another minute.

She was hit with a hailstorm of realizations. She wasn't going to have one friend at this school who wasn't in drama—even Candace, who was supposedly her friend already. She was never going to get invited to a party that wasn't a drama party. Unless Candace gave her another guilt invite. If she liked a boy who wasn't in drama, she wouldn't have a chance.

So I have a choice, Brynn thought. *Drama League or everything else.*

She pushed herself to her feet and walked into the auditorium, straight up to the front of the stage. "Mr. Saunders, can I talk to you?" she asked.

The drama advisor glanced up at her in surprise. "Can it wait until we're done with this scene?" he asked.

"No." Brynn knew she was being rude, but she couldn't wait. If she did, she would lose her courage. "This won't take long."

By now, everybody was watching. She could feel Drew's eyes on her from where he stood onstage. Brynn forced herself to ignore him.

"Okay. Everyone take five," Mr. Saunders called.

Nobody moved. Well, too bad. Brynn was just going to have to do this publicly. "I quit," she blurted out.

"What?" Rosemary cried from stage left.

"What?" Mr. Saunders echoed.

"I quit. I don't want to be in the play." The words tumbled out of Brynn's mouth. "I don't want to be in Drama League."

"What are you talking about? You love acting," Drew said, confused.

"And you're great at it," Rosemary added.

"What is this about, Brynn?" Mr. Saunders asked gently.

"Nothing. I just . . . I quit," she said. "I'm sorry."

Brynn turned and hurried up the aisle to the back doors of the auditorium, not looking back. If she looked back, she would see confused faces. Rosemary's and Drew's. Her peeps.

Brynn pushed through the double doors and hurried out into the school lobby. She turned right and went straight to the English wing. Wilton Academy clubs always put signs on their meeting rooms. She passed the Future Writers Club and the Wilton Poetry Jam and stopped at a classroom with a sign that said DEBATE CLUB.

Taking a deep breath, Brynn yanked the door

open and stepped inside. Everyone turned to look at her. *That's okay, just act like you're playing a role onstage,* she told herself. She lifted her chin and put a confident smile on her face as she walked over to the teacher, Ms. McAdorey.

"Hi. I'm Brynn. I was wondering if I could join the debate team," she said. "I hope it's not too late."

"Not at all," Ms. McAdorey replied. "Welcome aboard, Brynn."

"Thank you," Brynn replied. *Popularity, here I come!*

By the time the bell rang for lunch on Tuesday, Brynn was exhausted. She had been assigned the Boston Tea Party for her first practice debate, and she'd spent half the night reading about it. She had to argue the position that the Boston Tea Party was a criminal act, and she couldn't even imagine how to begin. It had taken her two hours just to memorize all the rules of debating—she hadn't even started studying the actual Boston Tea Party yet!

Brynn got in the lunch line and stared at the choices: chicken parmesan, veggie burgers, or grilled salmon. *I wish Rosemary was here,* she thought. *I have no idea what to eat.* It didn't seem likely that any school cafeteria was going to do a good job with grilled salmon, even an expensive school like Wilton Academy.

"What can I get you, honey?" the lunch lady asked.

"Um . . . a veggie burger, I guess," Brynn said. Hadn't Rosemary said they were decent the first day they had lunch together? She took her tray and headed out to the caf. Rosemary and Drew were sitting at the usual table, along with Eli and Trina.

There was an empty seat. *My seat,* Brynn thought. *But if I sit with the drama geeks at lunch, doesn't that still make me a drama geek, too?*

She had quit the play. Something she really loved. She didn't want it to be for nothing.

"Brynn! Hey!" Drew called, waving.

At almost the same instant, Joshua called her name. "Sit with us!" he added.

I quit drama and joined debate yesterday, and my life is already changing, Brynn thought. *I'm getting an invitation to sit at the table with all the most popular kids.*

"I've got to talk debate stuff," she told Drew as she took the empty seat next to Joshua. Only a few feet away from the drama table, but so, so far away.

Brynn tried to focus all her attention on the conversation going on around her. She didn't want to pay any attention to the little voice inside her that was saying she was a complete phony.

"All I'm saying is that it doesn't make sense for one teacher to grade on a curve if other teachers don't," Samantha told Allen.

"So you think that the kids who have Mr. Marter will have higher averages because they're graded on a curve?" Allen asked.

"Exactly. It makes the rest of us look bad."

"It does not," Allen said. "If anything, there will be fewer kids with As in Mr. Marter's class . . ."

"Maybe we should get those two onto the debate

team, huh, Brynn?" Joshua asked, leaning toward her.

"Yeah, they seem like naturals," Brynn replied with a smile. "They can't even stop debating to eat lunch."

"You call it debating, but it sounds like arguing to me," Candace said. "They're always arguing."

"We are not," Allen argued.

"Okay, that's the con side," Joshua said, winking at Allen. "You want to take the pro side, Brynn?"

"I don't know. I'm new at the whole debate thing. I might not be ready," Brynn joked.

Candace looked confused. "What are you guys talking about?"

"Brynn joined Debate Club with Joshua and me," Rowan put in, turning away from Allen and Samantha, who were starting up their argument again, this time about which one of them had spent more hours on their homework the night before.

"You joined Debate Club?" Candace asked. "What about Drama League?"

Brynn shot a look over at Drew and Rosemary's table. "I quit," she said.

"You quit?" Candace repeated. "You quit the play?"

"Yup," Brynn said.

Samantha raised her eyebrows, then gave a small nod of approval. "Smart move."

"Very smart. Debate Club is going to have a killer year," Rowan said. "We're stronger than we've ever been, and the toughest team we have to face is West Cohelton."

"And they lost their best debater," Joshua said. "She moved to Georgia. So they're totally beatable this year—as long as we're all at the top of our game."

"Well, I studied all night," Brynn said. "I'll be ready."

A burst of laughter interrupted them. Brynn turned to see Drew using the bun of his veggie burger like a mouth, making it talk to Rosemary. Rowan rolled her eyes, and Joshua went right back to talking about debate.

But Brynn couldn't help thinking that the kids at her old table were having a lot more fun than she was.

▲ ▲ ▲

Candace's head was spinning. It was Wednesday, and she'd only been at Rowan's house for an hour, but it felt like a whole day. *At least we're not talking about math*, she thought. Instead, they were studying history tonight.

The study group consisted of Candace, Rowan, Samantha, and Joshua. And this week, Brynn was there, too. Joshua and Rowan had asked her to join since they were all friends from Debate Club now.

"The point is, you can only judge history based on who wrote the stories," Brynn was saying. "If there's a war, whoever wins is the one who gets to write the history books. So all we learn is their side of the story."

"This is about the Boston Tea Party, isn't it?" Joshua teased her.

"Well, yeah," Brynn replied. "If the British had won the Revolutionary War, we would all learn about the Boston Tea Party like it was an illegal act. It was breaking and entering!"

"But we won," Candace put in. "So we learn about it like it was a great, heroic thing."

"Right," Brynn said.

"Did you know that in England they don't call it the Revolutionary War?" Rowan asked. "They call it the American War of Independence, and they don't really care about it very much."

"Did you learn that during your class this summer?" Samantha asked. Rowan had spent the summer in London with her cousins, and she'd taken a class at one of the local colleges.

Rowan nodded. "I learned so much stuff, you guys. I'm definitely doing an exchange summer during high school. I think it will really give me an advantage in my social studies classes."

"Maybe," Samantha said doubtfully. "I'd rather do a community outreach thing. You know, start up a local interest study group or something. I think that looks better on a college application."

"Yeah, but it's not all about college," Candace said. Her stomach was starting to ache. "It's also about learning. Isn't it?"

Chill, she told herself. *Spider plant, spider plant, spider plant.*

Thinking the words "spider plant" over and over was her new relaxation technique. It reminded her of the conversation she and Drew had had at her party. And that made her feel happy.

I wonder what he's doing right now, Candace thought.

"Sure it's about learning," Samantha said. "But

there's only so much you can learn in school. You have to branch out and try to find education in other places, too."

I can barely keep up with the education I'm getting at school, Candace thought. *Am I really supposed to spend every second of the day learning something new?*

"Wow. When are we supposed to relax?" Brynn asked, as if she had read Candace's mind.

"You're not," Joshua said seriously. "How can you get your best grades if you're relaxing? Especially when none of your competition is relaxing."

"Your competition?" Candace repeated. "You mean . . . your friends?"

Samantha, Rowan, and Joshua all laughed. "You're so sweet, Candace," Samantha said. "Of course we're all friends. But we still compete for grades, right?"

"Right." Candace felt a stab of pain in her belly. "You know what? I don't feel so well," she said.

"What's wrong?" Brynn asked, her brow wrinkled in concern.

"Do you need a glass of water or something?" Rowan asked. "You look really pale."

"No. No thanks." Candace took a deep breath. "I think I'd better just go home."

"But what about our history test on Friday?" Joshua asked. "We barely even got started studying."

"I know. You guys should do it without me." Candace stood up. It felt hard to get a breath. "I'm gonna go."

"Don't worry. You're so good in history," Samantha said. "You'll be fine even without the study group."

"Thanks." Candace headed for the door. *I might do fine on this test,* she thought. *But how am I going to survive the rest of the school year?*

Spider plant. Spider plant, spider plant, spider plant. SPIDER PLANT!

chapter

TEN

"Hi, Candace!" Janine Serpe called, passing by in the hall on Friday morning.

"Hi," Candace called back. She was glad to hear that her voice sounded normal, because she didn't feel normal. She felt nervous and embarrassed. But most of all she felt hopeful. If her plan worked, it would solve her biggest problem.

"Good morning," Brynn sang, appearing from behind her.

"Oh, hi!" Candace turned and smiled. "How's debate going? Rowan and Joshua rave about you."

"It's a lot of work. I miss things like—like sleeping, for one thing. But it's interesting, too." Brynn spun the dial on her locker.

"I'm glad you decided to join," Candace said. "It means I get to see you a lot more. At lunch and study group and everything. So listen, I have to ask you something," Candace said in a rush. She couldn't wait to get it out. As soon as Brynn said yes, everything would be better.

"Go ahead." Brynn looked at her curiously.

"Well, you know how you're really good in math?" Candace said. "I'm not. I hate math. Last year, my parents had to get me a tutor."

"Okay," Brynn said.

"So they paid the guy fifty dollars a week," Candace went on. "And I didn't learn anything. I just don't get it. I'm not good at math."

"Maybe he wasn't a good tutor," Brynn said.

"I think I'm just hopeless," Candace admitted. "But I have to get an A in math. I have to." The thought of having to bring home less than that made her belly contract.

Brynn sighed. "Everybody here wants to get As in all their classes. But somebody has to get the Bs and Cs, too. There's nothing wrong with a B."

"Tell that to my parents," Candace said. "Or my brother. He's great at math."

"Well, you're great in history, right?" Brynn said. "And English?"

"Yeah, I'm good at those subjects," Candace agreed. "But it's math that I'm worried about. So I have an idea. Instead of getting the tutor again, I'll pay you the fifty dollars a week."

Brynn's eyes widened. "Wow. Um, I'm good at math, but I don't know if I have time to tutor you. I mean, with all my homework and Debate Club . . ."

"No, I don't want you to tutor me," Candace said. "I'll pay you fifty a week if you just let me copy your math homework every day."

Brynn's mouth dropped open. "What?"

"Just let me copy your work," Candace said.

"Homework is seventy percent of our grade, and then I can just study extra hard for the tests. I'll have more study time if I don't have to worry about the daily homework."

"But . . . but that's cheating," Brynn said. "I can't do that."

"Just think about it, Brynn," Candace begged, hot acid flooding her stomach. She knew she sounded desperate. But she had to make Brynn say yes. It was the only plan she'd been able to come up with. It was the only way she could hope to pass math.

"No," Brynn said firmly. "I'm sorry, Candace. But no." She shut her locker and walked away.

▲ ▲ ▲

"I cannot believe my eyes," Drew said on Monday. "That's Brynn. In the library. At lunch. This is a very rare sighting."

"I think you're right," Rosemary replied. She squinted at Brynn, pretending to study her. "But what is she doing? She's far from her natural habitat. And she has no food."

Brynn couldn't help laughing at their fake hushed voices, the kind that announcers in nature shows used when they were talking about lions on the savanna or something.

"It's called studying," she told them. "You know, reading, taking notes, that kind of thing."

"She speaks!" Drew cried, pretending to be surprised. He plopped himself down in the chair across the table from Brynn. Rosemary sat next to him, then grabbed Brynn's notebook and pulled it over to look at it.

"Talking points," she read. "Establish that history is in the eye of the beholder. Winner writes the history books. Next, establish laws of British colonies—" She broke off and looked up at Brynn. "Wow. Boring."

"It's the Boston Tea Party. I'm on the Royalist side for my practice debate this afternoon," Brynn explained.

"Wow. Boring," Rosemary said again. Drew cracked up.

"Actually, I've never really thought about history this way before," Brynn said. "I always just memorized what the teachers told me. I never thought about whether all that stuff was true or not, or whether other people might think of it differently. It was only when I started figuring out how to debate that I realized there are two sides to every issue."

"Okay, so Debate Club has changed your life?" Rosemary asked.

"Well, yes," Brynn admitted. "It's made my life a lot more filled with studying and a lot less filled with fun. I spent the entire weekend reading everything I could find on the Boston Tea Party."

"Then you're due for a break," Drew said. "Come have lunch with us."

Brynn glanced back and forth between them. "Did you come to the library just to find me?" she asked, touched.

"Of course. We haven't seen you in days," Drew said.

"We were planning to kidnap you from the

popular table, but then you didn't even show up in the caf," Rosemary added. "This was the only other place we could think of."

"So here we are, and here you are," Drew said. "And we're all hungry and so we should eat." He grabbed Brynn's backpack. "Let's go. The lunch line is going to close in ten minutes."

"I can't." Brynn ran her hand through her hair, frustrated. "I'm sorry."

"Oh, come on," Rosemary said. "Look, we know you probably feel weird around us because you quit Drama League."

That's true, Brynn thought. *But mostly I feel weird around you because I'm trying not to be a drama geek like the two of you.*

"That's why we wanted to find you," Drew said. His voice was more serious than Brynn had ever heard it. "We just wanted to tell you that we're still your friends."

"Yeah. So you don't want to be in the play, so what?" Rosemary said. "We can still hang out. You can still eat lunch with us."

Brynn felt terrible. Rosemary and Drew were so cool. They didn't even care that she had completely messed up the play by quitting. They didn't care that she had ignored them and eaten lunch with Candace's friends for the past week. And they really didn't care if everybody else thought of them as freaky, geeky drama nerds.

"I would love to have lunch with you guys," she said truthfully. "But I can't. After school today is my first debate ever. And you know how competitive all the kids in the club are—they're all going to be super prepared. I have to be ready."

"You are ready," Drew told her. "You said you spent the entire weekend studying."

"Yup. No TV. No bike riding. No listening to music. Nothing but the Boston Tea Party," Brynn confirmed. "I mean, besides my regular homework."

"So you're ready." Rosemary stood up.

"No. I'm not. Joshua and Rowan can rattle off facts without even thinking," Brynn said. "I still have to look at my notes. You can't be a good debater if you're busy trying to find where you wrote some obscure fact. I have to memorize all of it." She paused and gulped in a breath. Her stomach had butterflies just thinking about the debate today. She felt seriously unprepared—even though she'd never spent so much time preparing for anything in her life!

I wonder if this is how Candace feels about math class, she thought. She still couldn't believe her friend had asked her to cheat like that. Candace must be having a really hard time.

Brynn looked back down at her pages and pages of debate notes. *It definitely is hard to fit in at this school,* she thought.

▲ ▲ ▲

"Brynn! You were amazing!" Joshua cried at the end of the practice debate after school that day. He raised his hand for a high five.

Just like Drew, Brynn thought as she slapped his

hand with hers. *But he's not nearly as funny as Drew.*

"Yeah, you really were." Rowan didn't sound as enthusiastic. She had been on the team that lost to Brynn and Joshua. "I can't believe that was your first debate ever."

She actually sounded suspicious. Brynn had to keep herself from rolling her eyes. At Wilton, people probably *would* lie about their experience—that way they would look smarter in a debate. "I spent all weekend studying," Brynn said. "Plus, I guess it was beginner's luck."

Rowan nodded.

"Congratulations, Brynn," Ms. McAdorey put in, reaching out to shake her hand. "With you on board, I have a feeling this debate season is going to be a winner!"

"Thanks," Brynn said.

Everyone was smiling and congratulating her. When people acted like that after she'd given a great performance in a play, Brynn felt on top of the world. But now, all she felt was relief that the debate was over with. She'd been seriously nervous about it, and while it was going on, all she could think about was trying not to mess up.

I might be good at this, she thought. *But I definitely don't love it. Not like I love acting.* Could she really spend her time at this school without ever standing under the stage lights? Without losing herself in a part? Without doing the thing she loved most?

Valerie logged on to the camp blog and gave a long, low groan. There were dozens of messages between Gaby and Chelsea. She decided to read the last ones first. That would probably give her the deets, and she wouldn't have to plow through the G & C tirades.

With another groan, Valerie clicked on the last message from Chelsea.

Posted by: Chelsea
Subject: Don't Even Bother

I SO EXTREMELY QUIT!!!!!

Oh great, Val thought. *Oh, so extremely great.* Although in a way, it might actually be easier to run the activity night without Chelsea. Just because without Chelsea, there wouldn't be so much Chelsea/Gaby battling.

Feeling a tiny bit better after this realization, she clicked on Gaby's last message.

Posted by: Gaby
Subject: You Know What?

I SO QUIT!!!!

Val shoved her desk chair away from the monitor so hard that the chair slammed into her bed. She almost got dumped onto the floor. It definitely would not be easier to do the activity night without

Gaby *and* Chelsea. It wasn't even close to being a one person job.

Maybe I can . . . negotiate a truce, Valerie thought. She decided the first thing she needed to do was figure out the cause of the latest fight. Sighing, she rolled her desk chair back over to her computer. She clicked on Chelsea's first message.

Posted by: Chelsea
Subject: Fab news for the HAFH team!

You won't believe what I've arranged for our activity night. I designed the coolest nametags for everyone. They are on braided cords that go around the person's neck. I just finished making all fifty of them.
You two can thank me later!

That wasn't too bad, Val thought. It wasn't cool that Chelsea had just gone ahead and actually made the nametags without showing her and Gaby the design or anything, but . . . Chelsea was Chelsea. Valerie clicked on Gaby's first message.

Posted by: Gaby
Subject: Uh . . .

Uh, Chelsea, sorry but your "coolest" nametags aren't going to work. I've already got team T-shirts for everybody. The nametags would hang down and cover the team logos I came up with. I guess if you want to just do the little pin-on nametags, that could be okay.

Yikes, Val thought. *Big, big yikes.*

She was about to click open Chelsea's reply when she got an IM from her. She clicked on the button to read the message.

<Chelsea1>: Did you see my post? I'm quitting.
<Valfrog>: Yeah, I saw it. I was thinking, maybe we could make the cords on your nametags shorter or longer. That way people could see the nametags and the logos that Gaby has on her shirts.

Before she got Chelsea's answer, Valerie was hit with an IM from Gaby. She opened it up in a new window.

<[GabyFaby]>: I just wanted to be sure that you know I'm not going to be at the activity night. I quit. You can thank Chelsea for that.

Before she could come up with a reply for Gaby, Chelsea's reply to Valerie dinged onto her screen.

<Chelsea1>: No way. I'm done with the nametags. If we take off the cords and replace them, it will fray the holes. And anyway, I quit. That's Q. U. I. T.

Valerie decided to try to reason with Gaby.

<Valfrog>: I have an idea on how to solve the nametag/T-shirt logo sitch. How about if people wear the shirts with the logos on the back? That would be cute.

<[GabyFaby]>: Why are we even talking about this? What part of quit don't you understand, Val?

Hopeless, Val thought. This is totally hopeless. I'm going to have to run the activity night alone. The scavenger hunt, the singdown, and the charades.

She swallowed so hard it hurt her throat. Would she be able to pull off the event all by herself?

chapter

ELEVEN

Candace walked slowly toward math class. She didn't have her math homework done. She was going to have to turn it in to Mr. Merrill incomplete. Incomplete! She'd never done that before—not in any class.

Her stomach went volcano as she thought about that. She could feel it spewing what felt like lava. Or was it magma? She couldn't remember. Was magma even a word? It was like her brains were dissolving. Pretty soon she wouldn't just be going down in math. She'd be at the bottom of the class in everything. Her family would probably ask her to change her last name. They'd be embarrassed to be associated with her.

That sent a giant blast of lava—magma?—through her belly. Candace wrapped her arms across her stomach. The pressure didn't help.

"Spider plant, spider plant, spider plant," she muttered. That didn't help either.

I feel bad enough to go to the nurse, she thought. Cool relief flooded through her. She really did feel bad enough to go to the nurse. No lie. And if she was at the nurse, she couldn't be in math class.

Candace turned around and quickly started walking toward the nurse's office. *My stomach hurts,* she mentally rehearsed. *Or would "I have a stomachache" be better? Or "My stomach is a volcano and I don't know exactly what's erupting from it"?*

She hadn't figured out exactly the best thing to say by the time she reached the door to the nurse's office. She hurried in anyway, hoping the right words would come to her. The first word out of her mouth was, "Brynn!"

Brynn was lying on one of the three cots in the nurse's office. She lifted her head. "Hey," she said, her voice flat.

Their last conversation rushed back to Candace. She and Brynn hadn't spoken since the day Candace had offered to pay Brynn to do her math homework. Make that the day Candace had tried to bribe Brynn to cheat for her.

Candace's face flushed, feeling nearly as hot as the lava—magma?—in her stomach. "So, um, what's wrong with you?" she asked Brynn.

"Stomachache," Brynn answered, staring up at the ceiling. "The nurse will be back in a minute."

"She'll be back in a minute?" Candace echoed. Would she ever stop doing that? Not that repeating things was her biggest problem at the moment. "I have a stomachache, too," she added as she sat down on the cot next to Brynn. "I get them all the time. At least during school."

"Just during school?" Brynn asked, turning her head to look at Candace.

"Yeah. I didn't get one stomachache over the summer. Weird, huh?" Candace replied.

"Not so weird," Brynn said.

"What do you mean?" Candace stretched out on the cot. It made her feel a little better.

Brynn raised her eyebrows. "You're the smart one. Haven't you figured it out?"

Candace just stared at her. She hadn't figured it out, whatever Brynn was talking about. "I'm not smart," she burst out. "I offered to pay you to do my homework. A smart person doesn't have to do that."

"I'm in your study group, remember?" Brynn asked. "I should know if you're smart or not. And you are. You're just having a hard time with one subject."

"I'm just having a hard time with one subject. But my brother and my parents are good at everything. So I'm definitely not as smart as they are," Candace explained.

"Well, somebody in your family has to be the dum-dum," Brynn joked.

Her words felt like a punch in Candace's stomach. Her already aching stomach.

Brynn must have seen the pain on Candace's face, because she reached over and touched Candace's arm. "Hey, I was just kidding around. Sometimes joking about stuff can make you feel better. That's why you get the stomachaches, you know?"

Candace felt her forehead get all wrinkly. "Huh?"

"Because you're so serious all the time. You're always stressed. You're not like that at camp. That's why you don't get stomachaches there. I think. It's not like I'm a doctor. I don't even play one on TV," Brynn said lightly.

"The stomachaches do always get worse when I'm trying to do math," Candace admitted.

"See?" Brynn said. "You're the most stressed when you're trying to do math. Stress equals stomachache."

"So does that mean you're stressed?" Candace asked.

Brynn frowned. "I thought I just ate my lasagna too fast. I was in a hurry to get to the library. But . . . this school is pretty intense. I've never had so much homework. And being on the debate team is like having another class. I have to do a ton of research."

"What do we do?" Candace shook her head. "How can you go to the Wilton Academy and not be stressed?"

"Hmmm," Brynn said. "Hmmm," she said again. Then she smiled. "I have two ideas. Second, I'm going to help you with math. We can have a mini, low-stress study group."

"Second? But what's first?" Candace asked.

Brynn's smile stretched into a grin. "First is a surprise."

▲ ▲ ▲

To: Rosemary, Drew, and Candace
From: Brynnwins@pc.com
Subject: Fun!

Hi guys,

     You are hereby invited to a battle of wit, skill, and craziness. Mostly craziness. Meet me on the front steps fifteen minutes before the first bell. There will be prizes. Please come. It'll be fuuuun! (Candace, if you don't, I'm withdrawing my offer of help. This is my first idea. The surprise.)

     –Brynn

▲ ▲ ▲

For the first time since she'd quit drama, Brynn was excited about getting to school. She spotted Rosemary and Drew standing on the steps. Yay! She hadn't been sure they'd show. She raced over to them.

"You two are the coolest!" she exclaimed. "I didn't know if you'd ever want to talk to me again."

"Us? We were sure you didn't want to talk to us again. We practically begged you to hang out, and you were all, 'no, no, no, I must study,'" Drew answered.

"We figured you'd just contracted the Wilton Academy Plague. The one where all you think about is homework," Rosemary added. "But when we got your e-mail, we thought maybe there was hope for you."

"Yeah. That e-mail was very *dramatic*. And you said there would be prizes," Drew said. "You did bring the prizes, right?"

"No worries." Brynn patted her bulging backpack.

"There's Candace," Drew said. "She's part of this whole mysterioso competition, right?"

"That's the real reason he's here," Rosemary teased.

"No it's not," Drew muttered, but his ears turned red.

Brynn stood on her toes and waved. "Over here, Candace." She waited until Candace had joined the group, then she unzipped her backpack and pulled out a small stuffed hamster wearing a ninja outfit. "This lovely creature is the grand prize. He will be awarded to whoever gets the most points during the competition."

Rosemary and Drew both burst out laughing. After a few seconds, Candace joined in.

"What *is* the competition, anyway?" Rosemary asked.

"I'll get to that. But first—" Brynn pressed the hamster's left paw. "Hwaaah!" the hamster cried out in a high voice. Then it started dancing. And singing "Everybody Was Kung-Fu Fighting."

"I just wanted you to see how special the grand prize is," Brynn said.

"I want it," Drew said. "I need it. I must have it!"

"Then let me tell you how you can win the fabulous, insanely talented hamster," Brynn said in her best game-show announcer voice. She pulled three bright yellow envelopes out of her backpack and presented one to Rosemary, one to Drew, and one to Candace.

Drew got his envelope ripped open faster than anyone. He pulled out a sheet of neon orange paper and began to read. "Blow bubbles in the hallway between classes—15 points. Wear a clown nose at lunch—15 points. If a teacher asks you a question and you know the answer but you say you *don't* know the answer—100 points. Talk to someone in pig Latin—10 points. Color in a coloring book during study hall—10 points."

"We've all learned to read, thank you," Rosemary joked, elbowing Drew in the side. He finished reading the list silently—but mouthed all the activities as he read.

"You have until the final bell to earn points. The hamster will be presented right here on these steps as soon as school is out," Brynn told them.

"I'm in," Rosemary said. "That little hamster is mine. There's only one problem. I forgot my coloring book and my bubbles."

"And I left my clown nose in my other pants," Drew said.

Brynn reached into her backpack again. She handed out small gift bags with everything Drew, Rosemary, and Candace would need to compete. She had a set of the supplies for herself, too. She wasn't going to let the others have all the fun.

"Excellent," Drew said. He stuck on the big, red, rubber clown nose. "Do I get bonus points if I wear it all day and not just at lunch?"

"No," Rosemary answered for Brynn. "The points on the list are the points you get. No bonus ones, or it isn't fair. Oh, and, just so you know, I've decided to change my name to Tamesala. I won't answer to anything else."

"Woo-hoo! That's twenty points for Rose—I mean Tamesala." Brynn applauded.

She noticed that Candace was being very quiet. The other two seemed to understand the whole contest right away. It was a way to make school fun, and they were onboard with that.

But what about Candace? Would she even try anything on Brynn's list?

▲ ▲ ▲

Candace shoved Brynn's gift bag into her locker. She wouldn't be needing it. There was no way she could do any of the things on the list. Her friends would check her into a mental institution. And anyway, she had to study.

She grabbed her history textbook—the only book she hadn't had to lug home for homework yesterday. The gift bag tipped over, and the red rubber clown nose rolled out of her locker and bounced down the hall.

Nobody noticed it. They were all too busy racing to class. Candace started to giggle. The nose just looked so funny bouncing along with all the Wilton Academy students in their neat little uniforms.

Candace's giggle upgraded to an actual laugh. It was a nose. It was bouncing. And nobody even glanced at it. The words Brynn had written at the bottom of Candace's list sprang into her mind: *Fun shouldn't be something you only have in the summer. Do this.*

As she stood there thinking, Drew hopped around the corner, blowing bubbles. He must have added the hopping just for more fun. He looked like he was having an amazing time. Even with people staring at him like he was stupid or crazy or both.

Fun shouldn't be something you only have in the summer. Do this.

I will, Candace decided. She left her locker door hanging open and chased after the bouncing nose. She started laughing again as she snatched it up.

"Candace?"

Candace glanced up to see Samantha and Joshua staring at her. "What *is* that?" Samantha asked.

Pig Latin, ten points, Candace thought. "An own-clay ose-nay," she replied. She stuffed the nose in her skirt pocket and went back to her locker.

"What did you just say?" Joshua called after her.

"A clown nose," Candace told him. "In pig Latin."

He looked at her blankly. So did Samantha.

"Pig Latin," she repeated. "Remember? From when we were little?"

"Oh. I guess." Samantha was frowning. "But why are you talking in pig Latin now?"

"Just for fun," Candace said.

They kept looking at her with confused expressions on their faces.

Wow, Candace thought. *I wonder if they're even capable of doing something just for fun.*

Was that how she seemed to Brynn? Was that the way she was during the school year—incapable of having fun?

Candace reached into Brynn's gift bag and pulled out the bubbles. Fifteen points for blowing bubbles in the hallway. She unscrewed the bottle, pulled out the wand, and blew a stream of perfect, shiny bubbles into the air. She didn't even wait for them to pop before she blew some more.

"Bubbles!" somebody yelled.

A boy passing by jumped into the air and stabbed one with his finger, laughing as it burst.

Candace grinned. So what if her friends thought she was nuts? She was having fun.

▲ ▲ ▲

"You should have heard Mr. Hannity ranting about how I was wasting my parents' hard-earned tuition money," Rosemary said at lunchtime. "Just because he asked me to define foreshadowing and I said I had no idea what it meant. I thought he was going to burst something, he was so horrified."

"That's crazy," Brynn commented. "Why did he even ask that question if he was so sure everybody knew the answer?"

"Yeah, that's crazy," Candace repeated. She didn't mean to keep repeating everything. But it *was* crazy.

"He thought it was a rhetorical question," Rosemary said, taking a big bite of her veggie burger. "And it was—who doesn't know what foreshadowing is?"

"Still, you did it. A hundred points for you." Brynn jotted it down in her notepad. "Nobody else has been brave enough to tell the teacher they don't know something."

Candace looked around the lunch table. She'd never eaten with anyone other than her popular friends before. And from the looks on their faces, they weren't at all pleased that she wasn't eating with them today.

But she was loving the change. Everything looked different from over here at the Drama League table. Of course, that could just be because she, Brynn, Rosemary, and Drew were all wearing red rubber clown noses.

"I'm going to do it next period," Drew announced. "I have math. I'm going to pretend I don't know the quadratic equation."

"I don't even have to pretend that," Candace cracked. "I really don't know it!"

They all laughed. "That doesn't count," Rosemary said. "You only get points for pretending."

Candace spooned some beef stew into her mouth. She sort of couldn't believe she'd just admitted out loud that she was having trouble in math. If she'd been sitting at her own table, she never would have said anything like that. Her friends would have been shocked, as if she was admitting a weakness or something. But Drew and Rosemary and Brynn didn't seem to care.

"I can't believe you're eating the beef stew," Drew said, peering into her bowl. "Rosemary—I mean Tamesala—swears up and down that it will give me an ulcer if I even let it onto my tray."

"It's true. I've never seen anybody eat the beef stew without getting sick," Rosemary agreed. "What's your secret?"

Candace glanced down at the nearly empty bowl on her tray. "I don't know," she said. "I usually don't eat this much of it."

"And your stomach doesn't feel like it's going to explode?" Rosemary asked.

"No." Candace hadn't even noticed her stomach all day today. She looked up at Brynn and smiled. "No. My stomach doesn't hurt at all."

△ △ △

"X equals 14," Candace announced after school that day. She squinted at her math notebook. "Doesn't it?"

"You bet it does," Brynn told her. "You did that problem in, like, thirty seconds. You didn't even have to think about it."

Candace leaned back in the library chair and stretched. "I know! It was almost easy. Like I knew what I was doing."

"So what changed?" Brynn asked. "Was it just my brilliant tutoring?"

"Well, I'm sure that helped," Candace said, laughing. "But . . . I don't know . . . I just wasn't worried about it for a change. I don't feel as stressed as usual."

"Okay, so it wasn't my brilliant tutoring. It was my brilliant plan for having fun," Brynn said. "You spent the day thinking about stupid things like clown noses and pig Latin instead of stressing about math."

"You're right. I didn't stress about math at all," Candace replied. "I feel totally relaxed."

"Good, that was the plan," Brynn told her seriously. "It's so cool that you did everything on the list, by the way. I wasn't sure if you would."

"I wasn't sure I would, either," Candace admitted. "It's easy to have fun at Camp Lakeview. But it never occurs to me to do anything fun during the school year. I guess I feel like fun isn't allowed, not when I should be thinking about my grades and my future."

"See, that's the thing. Fun and relaxation are a necessary part of life," Brynn replied. "If you never relax, you'll be so stressed out that you start doing a bad job at everything. Even things you're usually good at."

"How did you figure that out?" Candace asked.

"It's an acting thing," Brynn explained. "Acting is hard. So one of the things they teach you in drama is that you always have to be relaxed. If you're relaxed, you do a better job at the hard stuff. You can concentrate better because your brain isn't filled with all kinds of stressful thoughts."

"Is that why actors are always stretching out before performances, and playing games and stuff?" Candace asked.

"Yup. We have to stay loose." Brynn looked thoughtful. "And we have to learn not to let negativity in. You know, like if people say mean things or if they're unsupportive. Actors have to learn to let all that negative stuff roll off their backs."

"It sounds like you've learned about a lot more than acting in your drama clubs," Candace said. "And you're totally right. I've spent so much time worrying about what other people think that it's made me crazy. From now on, I'm not going to worry anymore about what anybody says. Even teachers and parents. In fact . . ." She stood up.

"Where are you going?" Brynn asked.

"I'm going to go do something pretty much all my friends would think was a bad idea. All my old friends, anyway!" Candace announced.

▲   ▲   ▲

I wonder what she's going to do? Brynn thought as she headed from the library to debate practice.

Joshua smiled and patted the desk next to him as she came in. "I found this incredible statistic about the amount of accidents caused by drunk drivers. Our team was unstoppable in the Boston Tea Party debate before. We're going to massacre in the debate about bringing back Prohibition."

Brynn pulled open her backpack, smiling as she saw a bottle of bubbles near the top. She took out her notebook and flipped it open. "I found some great stuff, too. Listen to this quote from Carrie Nation."

She pulled in a deep breath and began to read. "I felt invincible. My strength was that of a giant. God was certainly standing by me."

Brynn got to her feet. She couldn't stop herself. Suddenly she was Carrie. Getting ready to perform one of her *hatchetations*, whacking away at a saloon with a hatchet because she believed she was called by God to save men from drinking. She felt strong, and powerful, and a little bit crazy.

"I smashed five saloons with rocks before I ever took a hatchet," she continued, her voice rising with emotion and the strength of her convictions. Carrie's convictions!

"Wow," Joshua said. "That was . . . intense."

"Aren't you going to sit back down, Brynn?" Rowan asked.

Every person in the room was looking at her. And it felt good. It had felt even better to be Carrie for that brief stretch of time. She loved that about acting. How you actually slipped into someone else's skin. She couldn't believe she'd ever given this up.

"I think I should do the quote as Carrie in the debate. I think it would be a lot more powerful. And exciting," Brynn said, still on her feet. "I could read some of those quotes from mothers who had kids killed in drunk driving accidents in character, too. That would be—" She looked over at Joshua. "Now *that* would be intense. We'd blow everyone away." And Brynn would get to do the thing she loved more than anything in the world.

"I think it would distract from the points you are trying to make," Rowan said.

"Me too," Joshua agreed.

"It doesn't seem like an appropriate strategy to me," Serafina, one of the other debaters, offered from across the room.

"Just let me do one of the mom quotes in character," Brynn said eagerly. She couldn't wait to get onstage again. Well, sort of onstage.

"Brynn, you aren't listening. We don't think it's a good idea," Rowan said.

"But—" Brynn protested.

Joshua cut her off. "This isn't the Drama League, Brynn."

"You're right. It isn't," Brynn answered. "And that's the problem."

▲ ▲ ▲

Candace sat at the back of the auditorium, watching Drew sing to the man-eating plant. He was amazing. He gave it everything he had.

What's he going to say? she wondered. *Is it too late? Is he going to turn me down because I turned him down?*

Her life would be easier if he did. She wouldn't get any flack from her friends. She wouldn't have to worry about how she'd even find time to go to the movies with all her homework.

She wouldn't have nearly as much fun.

Drew finished his song, and Candace applauded until her hands tingled. When he leaped off the stage, she didn't give herself time to think. She walked right over to him. She didn't want to change her mind.

"Drew, um, hi," she said. She wished she were an actor like him and Brynn. Then she could just act like a girl who knew how to ask a boy out.

"Hey, Candace. You were awesome in Brynn's contest," Drew said.

Should she try to get the conversation around to movies? Then she could jump from there to asking if he wanted to see one?

"The most fun I had at my party was talking to you," she blurted out.

"Really?" Drew asked. "That's—really?"

"Drew, we need you up here again," the drama teacher called.

"I've gotta—" Drew took a step toward the stage.

Candace couldn't let him leave. If she didn't ask him now, she might never do it. "Stop!"

Drew froze. "Am I supposed to put my hands in the air?" he joked.

"No. No. I just . . . Do you want to go to the movies? With me?"

A grin spread across Drew's face. "Are you kidding?"

Candace shook her head. "I'm not good at that."

"Absolutely I want to go to the movies with you. Anywhere. Anytime," Drew answered.

"Drew! We're waiting!" the drama teacher called out.

"I've gotta—" Drew said. Then he leaned forward and kissed her on the cheek.

Samantha would die if she saw that, Candace thought.

And she didn't care at all.

"Feed me!" Rosemary was yelling as Brynn pushed open the door to the auditorium. "FEED ME!"

"Okay, let's take a quick break," Mr. Saunders called out. "Everybody back in ten. We'll start with Audrey and the dentist."

Drew leaped off the stage with a move worthy of a stuntman. He headed straight to the front row— where Candace was sitting—and plopped down beside her. They smiled at each other like they had the biggest, best secret.

And Brynn suddenly had a pretty good idea what Candace had done that she thought her friends—at least her old friends—would think was a bad idea. Good for her!

Brynn was getting ready to change her own life. If it wasn't too late. She made her way down the aisle to where Mr. Saunders was sitting, three rows back from the stage. He looked up and gave her a smile. "I didn't expect to see you here," he said.

"I know. Do you mind if I sit down?" Brynn asked.

"Of course not." The advisor moved a stack of script notes out of the way, and Brynn perched on the edge of the seat next to him.

"The plant looks good so far," she said.

"Yup. The art department makes us some more greenery every day. Soon enough we'll have the entire Audrey II." He narrowed his eyes at her. "But something tells me you're not here to talk about the sets."

"No." Brynn bit her lip. "I want to be back in the play," she burst out.

Mr. Saunders studied her face for a moment. "You know, Brynn, I had to give your part to somebody else," he said. "I can't take the role of Audrey away from Ana just because you've changed your mind."

"I know." Brynn couldn't help feeling a stab of disappointment. Still, she knew it wouldn't be fair to give her back the lead role after she'd acted like such a flake. "That's okay. I still want to be in the play. I'd be psyched just to be part of the chorus. I just want to be involved."

"You really love it, don't you?" the advisor asked. "Drama?"

"I do," Brynn confirmed. "Acting is my favorite thing in the whole entire world. And I'm not going to stop doing it just because some people think it's stupid or uncool."

"Then I'd say you've learned a valuable lesson about sticking to your guns," Mr. Saunders told her. "Welcome back to Drama League, Brynn."

Brynn let out a whoop of pure joy. "I'm a drama geek again!" she shouted.

"All right!" Drew yelled.

"She's back. Our Brynn is back!" Rosemary called.

The rest of the kids in the auditorium gave her a round of applause. Candace hurried over to her. "I know I'm the one who said you should go out for debate, but I was wrong. You love drama. It makes you happy. You shouldn't give it up for anybody."

"And what about you? Does it make you happy hanging with Drew? I saw you sitting with him," Brynn answered.

"Yeah. It makes me happy, happy, happy!" Candace said. "I don't know if I'll ever be able to eat lunch with my friends again, but I'm still happy."

"There's always a place for you at the drama table," Brynn told her. "We might not be popular. But we have fun!"

chapter

TWELVE

"Have you decided yet?" the man at the mall taco stand asked Gaby on Saturday afternoon. He was tapping his finger impatiently, but she saw no reason to hurry. Why should he care if she took a long time figuring out which value meal to eat? It's not like he had anywhere else to go. His job was to wait on people. Now if there were people behind her in line at the food court taco stand, *then* she would have a reason to hurry. Because it wouldn't be nice to make other customers wait. And Gaby was a nice person.

No matter what Chelsea thought.

"Um . . ." she said. "I think I'm going to have the number three."

"Bad choice," a boy said from behind her. "The refried beans here stink. You should go for the number two, and then just add some Spanish rice on the side."

Uh-oh, Gaby thought. *Was there somebody behind me this whole time and I didn't realize it?* She put a friendly smile on her face and turned to the boy.

"Leland," she said, her smile vanishing.

"You're Leland. From Home Away From Home."

"Actually, I think this taco place is my true home away from home," he replied. "Hola, Pedro."

"Hola, señor Leland." The taco guy smiled at him. "You want your regular?"

"Not today. I think I'm going to try something new," Leland said. "Hit me with the Hot Hot Chili taco."

The taco guy whistled. "Bold move."

"And whatever my friend here wants," Leland added.

Pedro raised his eyebrows, looking at Gaby. "I'll do the number two with Spanish rice on the side," she told him. "Thanks for the suggestion," she added to Leland.

Pedro slid a tray over the counter and Leland handed him a few dollars. "I'll grab the drinks," Gaby offered. She picked up the two large cups and followed Leland over to an empty table in the crowded mall food court.

"Thanks," Gaby said. "For lunch. You really didn't—"

"Look, I was totally rude to you the other day," Leland cut her off. "The least I can do is buy you a couple of tacos."

Gaby knew her mouth was open, but she couldn't think of anything to say. She was too surprised. So she took a bite of her taco.

"Anyway, I'm sorry," Leland went on. "I know you were there to help out and I was a brat. I just . . . I was worried. My little brother came back from chemo that day and he was super sick all afternoon. I just didn't feel like being nice."

"Okay," Gaby said.

"I was upset and I took it out on you."

"That's all right," Gaby said. She couldn't believe he was apologizing to her. She had thought she was the one who had been rude. "Sometimes I don't feel like being nice, either."

He chuckled.

"So let's start over," she suggested. "I'm Gaby."

"Hi, Gaby," Leland said. "It's nice of you to volunteer at Home Away From Home."

"Thank you," she said. "I really want to help. I'm trying to be a nicer person."

"Nicer than what?" Leland asked.

"Well . . . I haven't always been the sweetest girl to be around," Gaby admitted. "Some of my friends let me know that I could be kind of a pain."

"You can't be that bad," Leland said. "You're volunteering at the Home. You and your friends are running the activity night tonight, right?"

Gaby made a face. "Uh, not really," she admitted.

"What do you mean?" Leland asked around a bite of his chili taco.

"We were supposed to run the activity night," Gaby said. "But my friends are so annoying! I mean, it was my idea to volunteer there in the first place. So I should get to be in charge, don't you think? And then they didn't want to do what I wanted to do and they kept trying to take over. Especially Chelsea. She's the blond one. She's totally bossy."

Leland didn't say anything. He just kept eating.

"Like, for tonight we finally agreed that there would be a three-part competition, and everyone would be divided up into teams," Gaby went on. "So I got T-shirts for all the kids that said what their teams would be. Then Chelsea makes these nametags that hang right over the T-shirt logos I designed."

Leland finally finished his taco. He looked up at her. "Are you serious?"

"Yes!" Gaby cried. "Can you believe her? So anyway, I quit. She's such a jerk. I'm not going to work with her."

"Wow. I guess maybe I wasn't too hard on you the other night," Leland said. "You're unbelievable."

"Me?" Gaby gasped. "Chelsea is the one who—"

"I don't care." Leland stood up. "You're really going to ditch Home Away From Home over a bunch of nametags and T-shirts? Do you just not even realize that the people at the Home have *real* problems, Gaby?"

"Of course—"

"We don't care about stupid shirts," he interrupted. "All we want is a few hours of fun to take our minds off the fact that our brothers and sisters are sick. Really sick. My baby brother might die, Gaby. Did you even think about that when you were making your little T-shirts?"

Gaby noticed that her mouth was hanging open again. She shut it. There was nothing she could say. Leland was right. She had been acting like a complete selfish jerk, while the people she was supposed to be helping were busy struggling with serious problems.

"Enjoy your lunch," Leland said. Then he turned and stalked off.

He'd probably be happy if he never saw me again, Gaby thought. *Because I'm the worst volunteer, and the most UN-nice person ever.*

▲ ▲ ▲

"What time do you need to be at Home Away From Home tonight, sweetheart?" Chelsea's dad asked as she walked by the den on her way to her bedroom.

Chelsea paused in the hallway. She hadn't told her parents that she had decided to quit volunteering. And now, looking at her father's proud, smiling face, she couldn't bear to tell him the truth. "Um, let me go check the schedule," she said. Then she bolted for her room and closed the door behind her.

Her dad had gone through so much. His cancer was in remission, and all the doctors said that his prognosis was good. But he'd lost so much time to his illness. How could she tell him that she'd just bailed on the whole helping-people thing? Especially when her volunteering made him happy?

Chelsea glanced around her room, looking for something to take her mind off the fact that she was not busy getting ready for activity night tonight. Her gaze fell on her diary, which was sticking out from underneath her pillow.

"That will help," Chelsea murmured. It always made her feel better to write things out. Somehow her problems seemed less awful once she had poured out her feelings in the diary. She flopped down on her bed, pulled out the book and a pen, and opened to the first blank page.

Dear diary,
I'm supposed To be helping people TonighT, buT Gaby was so annoying ThaT now I'm noT.

That sounded pretty lame.

She kepT Trying To Take conTrol oF The whole volunTeering experience. JusT because iT was her idea. BuT I'm The one who Knows whaT iT's like To have sickness in The Family. I'm The one who undersTands whaT The people aT Home Away From Home are going Through.

Chelsea stopped writing. Her heart was pounding hard. She stared at the words she'd just scrawled, and suddenly they began to swim in front of her eyes.

I don't want to cry, she thought, wiping away the tears that were forming.

She reached out and flipped back through her

diary until she found an entry from last year.

Dear Diary,

I'm scared. I'm so scared. All The Time, even when I'm asleep. I can Tell because I wake up and I still feel Tired. I Think I spend all night dreaming about what will happen if Dad doesn't get better. And at school, my friends Talk To me, but I don't really listen To Them anymore. All I can Think about is Dad and his cancer. The only Time I feel better is when I just veg out in front of The TV because I don't have To Think. But lately even That doesn't work very well.

Please please please let This experimental TreaTment work. Please let my father be okay again. I'll do anything. Just please let iT work.

It's okay, she told herself. *He's okay*. When did she stop waking up saying thank you for that? When did it start feeling almost ordinary that he'd recovered?

Chelsea closed the diary. Her throat hurt, and she tried to swallow down the lump that had formed there. Sometimes she forgot how bad it had been when her father was so sick. Sometimes she got sucked into being the same old selfish Chelsea that she had been before.

The Chelsea who cared more about nametags than about people.

Those kids at Home Away From Home feel just like I did, she thought. *They could just as easily have written that diary entry about their brothers or sisters.*

She did know how they felt. And she was supposed to be helping them, not hiding in her room because she was mad at Gaby.

"Have a good night, honey," Val's stepmother said as Val got out of the car in front of Home Away From Home. "Your mom will be by to pick you up at nine thirty."

"Thanks, Sharin," Valerie said. She turned and trudged up to the door of the huge house. It was pretty much impossible for her to have a good night, she knew. This was basically going to be the most humiliating night of her life. She would have to try to run a huge activity night for a bunch of kids all by herself, and she was worried that she couldn't do it.

I have the props for the scavenger hunt, she thought. *And I have all my cards for charades. As for the singdown, I'm just going to have to wing it.*

She was as prepared as she could be. But it wasn't enough, and Val knew it. There were just too many events, and too many teams, and only one Valerie. How was she supposed to oversee three things at once?

Emma and Samuel burst out the front door. "Valerie! What are we going to do tonight?" Emma called as she and her brother skidded to a stop in front of Val.

"You said it was going to be something awesome. What is it?" Samuel exclaimed.

"You'll just have to wait and see," Valerie told them. "But I'll tell you this. Part of it involves marshmallows. That's all the info you're getting."

"Cool!" Emma said. She and Samuel raced toward Home's playground.

I'm going to do the best I can. Emma and Samuel and all the other kids are counting on me, she told herself.

Val took a big gulp of air and pushed open the heavy door. Inside, little kids were running around the lobby. Older kids stood in little groups, talking. The place was packed. Everybody was gathered for activity night.

Manny wandered by in a bright orange T-shirt that said "Home Rangers" on it with a drawing of the Lone Ranger underneath.

"Cool shirt," Valerie said.

"Yeah, I was supposed to be a Home Fires. But I made them switch me to Rangers. The Fires T-shirts are pink," Manny answered, heading toward a table where cupcakes had been laid out.

It sounded very much like he was talking about

team T-shirts! A tiny bit of hope spiraled through Valerie.

"Manny!" she called after him. "Where'd you get the shirt?"

"Dining room," he answered, the words muffled by a large bite of cupcake.

Was Gaby in the dining room? She pretty much had to be, didn't she? Unless there was a T-shirt fairy, cousin to the tooth fairy, that her parents had never told her about.

Manny turned away from her to grab a second cupcake, and Valerie saw a loop of braided cord dangling from his back pocket.

Now hope was zinging through her. She very much suspected that the cord was attached to a nametag. And unless there was a nametag fairy . . .

Valerie didn't finish the thought. She dashed into the dining room. Neat rows of T-shirts and nametags were lined up on the long wooden table. And behind the table—

Chelsea and Gaby.

"We figured out a way to make the T-shirts and nametags work together," Gaby announced calmly, as if she hadn't had a fit and quit.

"We combined them!" Chelsea said happily, as if she also hadn't had a fit and quit.

"It was your suggestion," Gaby put in. "We just made the nametags shorter. Chelsea figured out that if we loop the cords twice, the nametags will be short enough that they won't cover the team logos."

"And you don't have to redo the cords and fray

the holes," Val guessed.

"Exactly."

"Great. But back up. I thought you guys weren't coming," Val said.

Chelsea and Gaby exchanged a look. "We weren't," Chelsea replied. "But then I realized that I was supposed to be helping these kids because I really understand what they're going through."

"And I realized that being nice means thinking about other people, not about myself," Gaby said.

"And we both realized that we had completely dumped this whole thing on you, and that's really not fair," Chelsea added. "Will you forgive us?"

"Are you kidding?" Val replied. "You're here to help. This is better than I could possibly have hoped! With the three of us running it, tonight will be the best activity night in the history of Home Away From Home!" She held out her arms, and the other two grabbed her in a group hug.

"So let's get started," Chelsea said.

"Just one minute," Gaby replied. "I have to find a guy named Leland."

"Leland Keyes?" Chelsea asked. "His shirt and nametag are right there on the end."

"Great." Gaby snatched them up. "I want to give these to him personally. Now that I've apologized to you two, I have to apologize to him." She hurried out into the lobby.

Val turned to Chelsea. "I'm really glad you guys came," she said. "I don't think I could have done this without my Camp Lakeview team!"

chapter

Posted by: Candace
Subject: Boys and Bs

Hi, everyone!

I can't believe I'm about to say this, but I need some advice on my love life! I asked a boy out. Yes, me! His name is Drew and he's supercute. You can ask Brynn—she's the one who introduced us. He's funny and nice and he is the star of the school play. I think I might really like him! So anyway, what am I supposed to talk about on a date? What am I supposed to wear? Does anyone have tips on how to impress a boy?

Drew isn't the only good thing going on for me, though. I also got a B on a math quiz today!! And I'm happy about it. Me—happy about a B! I didn't tell any of you this—but I had a really hard time in that subject last year, so I've been majorly stressed out about my grade this year. Lucky for me, the drama queen Brynn helped me straighten out my priorities and now I'm doing okay in the class. I might really be starting to understand algebra, I think. (It's easier to understand than boys!)

My parents weren't too thrilled with my B. But then I admitted to them that I was so afraid of failing that I offered to pay my friend to let me copy her homework. They backed right down—the B may not be the best grade ever, but at least it's truly my own grade. I don't think they realized how much pressure I was feeling about school.

Anyway, now that school is under control, I'm stressed about my date! In a good way. So send me all your dating stories and help me figure out what to do!

Posted by: Val
Subject: So. Much. Fun.

Shouting out to all my Camp Lakepuke buds!

You guys will never believe how amazing our Home Away From Home activity night was last week! The team of Chelsea, Gaby, and Val rules! Seriously? The singdown that we held for the siblings of the sick kids was—no joke—even better than the singdowns at camp. I think it's because everyone had gotten so into the first two events (scavenger hunt and charades) that they were all totally bonded by the time we reached the singdown portion of the evening. Gaby did an amazing duet with this cute boy named Leland, too. Is love in the air?

Anyway, we're all onboard for another activity night. We've already started planning it. But first we're going to help cook a meal. And then we're going to help expand the playground at the Home. I'll post pics of us three in our tool belts!

Posted by: Gaby
Subject: Re: So. Much. Fun.

Val said it all! We organized the best activity night in the history of the world, I think. Okay, maybe not. But it was definitely in the top ten!

As for Leland, maybe love is in the air. Who knows? Right now I'm just trying to be a good friend to him. His little brother is really sick, and Leland needs someone to talk to. And you know what? Even though I'm there to be nice to Leland, it makes me feel better, too.

Who knew that being nice was a way to make yourself feel good?

(I know, you all knew that, didn't you?)

Posted by: Chelsea
Subject: Re: So. Much. Fun.

I'm so glad I can be here for Gaby, to show her how to be nice. LOL.

Seriously, though, our activity night was a huge big deal for me. I can't believe I almost blew it by being so competitive. Just the looks on the faces of all those kids almost made me cry. They were having such a good time! I just know that they weren't thinking of their sick siblings, at least for a little while. For a couple of hours they got to be normal kids having a good time instead of family members worrying about someone they love.

You guys all know how sick my dad was last year. I remember how important it was to me to get my mind off of his illness sometimes. That's part of why I loved camp so much. It was a place that was all about friends and fun, and it kept me from worrying every single second of every day.

I feel like Gaby and Val and I were able to do that for the kids at Home Away From Home. It was truly amazing. I can't wait to do it again!

Posted by: Brynn
Subject: Popularity = overrated

What's up, everybody!

I have an announcement to make. I am a drama geek. There. I said it. I'm a geek and I love it! The kids at my new school think acting is for weirdos, and they think being totally competitive about grades makes you cool. Well, I tried to be that way, too. I wanted to be popular.

Actually, I wanted to be super-popular.

So I quit Drama League. And I had the lead role in the school play! But I quit anyway, just so I wouldn't get called a geek. I joined Debate Club, and I rocked it. (You all know I'm good at arguing. LOL.) But you know what? It was no fun. At all.

What's fun? Acting! Even if I'm not the star of the play anymore. At least I'm back in the play and back to doing what I love. Because who wants to be popular if it means turning into somebody else—somebody who's no fun?

So thank you for all your advice about starting my new school. I have a new school, and new friends, and a new outlook. But I'm still the same old Brynn!